PURRFECT DEMONS

THE MYSTERIES OF MAX 65

NIC SAINT

PURRFECT DEMONS

The Mysteries of Max 65

Copyright © 2023 by Nic Saint

Edited by Chereese Graves

www.nicsaint.com

Give feedback on the book at: info@nicsaint.com

facebook.com/nicsaintauthor
@nicsaintauthor

First Edition

Printed in the U.S.A

PURRFECT DEMONS

Of Mischief and Mice

It was a dark and stormy night when our house was visited by a mouse, requiring our urgent assistance in a matter of life and death. The thing is that it's not easy to garner sympathy for the plight of mice, who are not a popular species, so we had a hard time convincing Odelia to do something. But soon a special committee was formed to look deeper into the matter. Unfortunately the committee members were too busy battling their inner demons to bother with saving a colony of mice. And so in the end it was up to us to put our best paw forward and show them how things are done.

CHAPTER 1

The rumble of thunder hung in the air when Barry Spence decided to head into the office to finish an important presentation. He shouldn't be out on a stormy night like this, and obviously it was a bad idea. But since he was a conscientious man and he hated disappointing his employer, he kissed his wife and kids goodnight and got into that car anyway.

Allison told him not to go, since the weather forecast said it was going to be a big one, but Barry being Barry he figured he'd get to the office, located on the other side of town, before the storm hit, and then he'd simply put in a couple of hours before heading home again. By that time the worst of the storm would be over, and at least he'd be able to sleep safe in the knowledge that he'd gotten a head start on the next week.

His wife had told him he was crazy, and she had also told him he was a workaholic and should probably see a shrink if he kept this up, lest he wanted to have a heart attack at age fifty and leave his wife a widow and his kids without a father.

But he'd simply smiled at her, kissed the tip of her nose and told her he was invincible and he would never die.

Unfortunately the weather forecast had been off by about half an hour, and when Barry did indeed hit the road and passed the off-ramp, lightning struck a tree, a branch about as thick as Barry's leg splintered off and hit his car, causing it to careen off the road at a high rate of speed. He crashed into the now limbless tree and was killed on impact.

Or at least that's how it felt to him when his airbag blew up and he took the brunt of the impact. When he came to, firemen were working on the car, the Jaws of Life being used to prize open the door so they could get him out. A kindly-faced fireman told him to remain calm, and he would have told him he was calm. In fact he was about as calm as it gets. But before he could get the words out he lost consciousness once more.

The dream he had was a little bizarre. He was in a hospital being fussed over by a kindly nurse dressed in white, and when he asked her if she wanted to marry him, she laughed and told him to be good. "But I am good," he told the nurse. "I've always been good, that's the problem. I've probably been too good, which is why I'm in this mess right now."

When he finally opened his eyes he felt as if he was crawling his way back to the surface after having been lying at the bottom of a very deep dark pit. The nurse standing next to him and fiddling with the machines that monitored his vital signs was exactly the same nurse he'd seen in his dream, and when he blinked and tried to speak, she smiled and said, "Glad to see you're back, Mr. Spence. Now just rest and don't try to talk. I'll tell the doctor that you're awake."

He would have asked her if she was married, and if she was, was she his wife, but the fuzziness in his head finally subsided to such a degree he realized he must have been dreaming, and so he shut up with a touch of mortification, hoping he hadn't actually spoken those words to this nurse, and lay back against the pillow awaiting the arrival of the doctor.

When he glanced down, he saw he was pretty banged up, surrounded by machines of all shapes and sizes, blinking and beeping away to their heart's content. A bouquet of flowers stood on the bedside table and he wondered who had put it there since he couldn't see a sign of a card.

Before long, the door to his room opened again and a man strode in with purposeful steps. This could only be the doctor, he determined immediately. At least the man looked exactly like what he imagined a doctor would look like, and wouldn't have been out of place on an episode of *Grey's Anatomy*.

"Mr. Spence," said the man, his entire presence purveying a sense of importance and professionalism. "How are you feeling?"

"Groggy," said Barry. "So what happened to me, Doc?"

"You don't remember?" asked the doctor with a touch of concern.

"I…" He tried to think back, which gave him a shooting headache, but at least some blurred imagery from the accident came back to him. "I hit a tree," he said finally. "They had to cut me out of my car."

The doctor's frown deepened. "It's true that you were in a car accident," he said briefly.

The nurse he had proposed to—at least in his dream—had returned to the room and stood quietly and attentively by while the doctor explained Barry's predicament.

"So… how bad is it?" he asked as he touched his teeth with his tongue to ascertain if they were all still there.

"You broke a few bones and you took a pretty bad beating, so you can count yourself lucky to still be alive."

And as the doctor rattled off the list of ramifications of

the accident he'd been in, all Barry could think of was his wife and kids, and where they could possibly be. In the movies the moment the patient woke up after having been through hell and back, his wife and kids stormed into the room to throw themselves around the neck of their beloved relative. But in this case all he could see was this doctor and the nurse.

"So…" He swallowed with difficulty. "Where is my wife?"

Silence greeted him, and the doctor exchanged a look of concern with the nurse, who offered Barry the most compassionate look he'd ever been subjected to.

"My wife?" he repeated. "And the kids? Do they know what happened to me? Have they been told?"

"The thing is, Mr. Spence," said the doctor after a pause, "that your wife was also in the same accident you were in, and so were your kids. You may not remember this, but they were in the car with you. And I'm afraid they didn't make it."

For a moment he simply stared at the man. "I don't understand. I was alone in that car. I distinctly remember. I had to go into the office because I wanted to finish work on an important presentation and I thought I could head off the storm. Allison told me I shouldn't go but I didn't listen, which I now regret, of course. So you see, there's no way she could have been in the car with me, since I was alone. It was just me."

"You weren't going into the office, Mr. Spence," said the nurse now, adopting a kindly tone. "And you weren't alone. Your family was in that car with you. So when your car went off the road…" She eyed him with compassion. "You were thrown from the car, which went into the lake."

He stared at her, not comprehending. "I don't understand what you're saying," he said. "It's impossible. I'm telling you that I was going into the office." He smiled weakly. "My wife calls me a workaholic, and even keeps telling me this habit of mine to put work before everything else will be the death of me one day. Well, I guess she was right. Almost."

The doctor and the nurse had listened to this with stoic faces that nevertheless couldn't hide their concern.

"I think you better rest now, Mr. Spence," said the doctor. "It's going to take you a while to get back on your feet, so you better take it easy." He turned to the nurse, and gave her some instructions. For a moment Barry stopped listening, as he thought back to his wife's face when she implored him not to go out into that storm. The memory didn't jibe with what the doctor and that nurse were trying to tell him. Finally he tuned back in. "So… where is my wife?" he asked. "And when can I see her?"

At this point the nurse went a little pale and the doctor's face turned into an impassive mask. Which is how he knew they were probably telling him the truth, hard as it was to believe. Frankly it was impossible. It simply couldn't be. But as he thought about what had happened some more, he realized that his mind was playing tricks on him. And that maybe, just maybe, there was some truth to what these people were saying.

He still didn't believe it, though. How could he? If he did, it meant his life was effectively over, and even if technically it wasn't, the pain would be such that it might as well be. So he decided they were wrong. Allie simply hadn't been told, or else she was visiting her parents and couldn't be reached.

And as his mind flashed back to the day he and Allison got married, he closed his eyes and a smile curled his lips. It had been a sunny day, and his bride-to-be had been beautiful beyond anything he'd ever seen. So beautiful in fact that for perhaps the first time in his life he had wept like a baby.

He wept now, and wondered what his life was going to be

like from now on. He couldn't imagine it was going to look like anything much. One thing was for sure. Barry the workaholic husband and father was definitely a thing of the past.

CHAPTER 2

The streets were deserted and a heavy drizzle had turned them into a slick patch that made them all but impassable. Yet still one creature, in spite of everything, stirred as it stuck its nose from behind a car tire and peered out at the diffuse light distributed by a lone lamppost. The creature sniffed the wet air appreciatively, glanced left and right to ascertain whether its predators were safely hiding from the harsh conditions, and then ventured out from behind the safety of its hiding place. In one prolonged burst of speed it traversed the distance between the car and the lamppost, then up the pole until it had reached the safety of the top of the lamp, and triumphantly crowed with delight.

Not that it actually produced a sound, since that would have been tantamount to giving its enemies a clear indication of its position. The battle cry had been fully internalized, but the creature still pumped its little fist in a blatant gesture of defiance at a hostile world. As it glanced down at the pavement below, it was surprised suddenly to see a man standing there, his head covered with a cap and dressed in a yellow raincoat, collar up against the wind. At the foot of the man another creature sat, which could only be identified as a dog. The dog had lifted its hind leg and was doing its business against the lamppost, leaving a glistening puddle of moisture, before taking a tentative sniff and, satisfied it had done what it had ventured out to do, gave a soft woofle.

The man glanced down, growled something under his breath, and walked away, the dog happily prancing behind him, sniffing here and there as dogs do.

The creature lurking atop the lamppost wondered about the relationship between man and beast, and why the dog would voluntarily allow the man to put a leash on him and walk him around as if he owned him. Then again, the creature knew that the human-canine bond is a complicated one, and can only be plumbed to its fullest depth by an experienced professional of the human/canine mind. Freud, if he had lived, would probably be all over the study of this bond, as it might yield insight into the human psyche and what its urgent problems entailed.

The creature now settled on top of the lamppost, which was warm from the heat of the lamp, and quite comfortable, in spite of the drizzle that was still coming down in sheets of rain. And as it settled in for the duration, it fastened its beady little eyes on the house across the street, the real target of this expedition. The mission wasn't without peril, but it was also necessary. For in that house the greatest cat detective that had ever lived resided. And if the creature wasn't mistaken, events that would soon come to pass would demand the utmost of this investigator of crimes against the animal kingdom. It had a mission in mind for Max, as the feline sleuth's name was, but before it could approach the famous detective, it first had to screw its courage to the sticking point. And to that purpose the creature half-closed its eyes and rehearsed once again the speech it was going to launch into once it stood before Max.

Lives depended on it. In fact the fate of an entire community was at stake. And it all came down to this furry little hero.

* * *

IT HAD BEEN QUITE a turbulent week, I must say. Grace had been sick with a toothache these last couple of days, so much so she had to see a doctor—which wasn't difficult as her doctor lived right next door and was in fact her grandfather. Odelia had caught some bug and had been sick in bed with it, and then Chase had come down with the same bug just when Odelia was starting to feel a little better. But then I guess it's often that way. These things seem to come together, and hit you when you're reeling. The only ones who hadn't caught any bug were the four of us: Max (that's me), Dooley (my best friend), Harriet (our prissy Persian friend) and Brutus (Harriet's butch black mate). Not that we were complacent about it, since we all know that when you start crowing that your health is as well as it has ever been, you come down with something and usually it's something pretty nasty and debilitating. And since Vena the vet is just about our least favorite person in the world, the last thing we needed was to catch whatever bug was plaguing our humans and be forced to be subjected to Vena's particular brand of torture.

And so we simply took a wait-and-see approach to these events as they unfolded and hoped and prayed for the best, as one does.

A bout of bad weather had hit Hampton Cove hard, and was whipping up the ocean and flagellating the streets and houses of our small town, so much so that we had actually refrained from venturing out of the house these past couple of days and had no plans to go out for as long as this storm kept hovering over the area like a miasma.

Most storms are of the 'hit and run' variety: they pop up out of the blue, do their worst, and pop off again, like thieves in the night. But this one seemed to enjoy our misery, and showed no signs of beating a hasty retreat. Instead it kept hanging around like an unwelcome visitor, eager to wreak as much havoc on Hampton Cove's population as possible. Almost as if it had a mind of its own, which of course is ludicrous.

Still, as we glanced out of the window at the street outside, we could see neighbors taking their dogs for a walk with as much reluctance as they could muster.

"Why would dogs go out in this storm, Max?" asked Dooley. "Don't they want to stay nice and warm inside like we do?"

"It's their bladders," Brutus ventured. "The dog itself, as a creature, wants to stay nice and warm, but its bladder prevents it from enjoying life. It keeps pushing the dog to go outside so it can relieve itself from the excess fluid against trees and lampposts. Just like Rufus is doing now."

Rufus, the sheepdog belonging to our next-door neighbor Ted Trapper, didn't even seem bothered all that much by the conditions to which he was being subjected. Contrary to his owner, there was an actual spring in his step as he raised his hind leg against a willing lamppost and did his business. Ted, on the other hand, seemed to hate every minute of it. But then that's the price one pays when one becomes the proud owner of a dog: to head out in all manner of weather to accommodate your canine.

"If I were Ted I would teach Rufus how to use a litter box," said Harriet. "Just saying. It would be so much more convenient."

"It would definitely make his life a lot easier," I agreed. "But the fact of the matter is that dogs don't like litter boxes. And also, I don't think they make litter boxes for dogs the size of Rufus. That thing would almost have to be as big as the doghouse that Ted built in his backyard."

"So?" said Harriet. "There's your solution right there. Ted should simply turn that doghouse into a litter box and all his problems would be solved. Rufus never uses that thing anyway, so it's just a waste of space."

She was right that Rufus hardly ever used the doghouse Ted had once constructed in a frenzy of activity. Rufus spent most of his time indoors, and when he did venture out he much preferred to prance around the backyard instead of exploring the limited space of his doghouse.

"Rufus is getting awfully wet," said Dooley with a touch of concern lacing his voice. "If this keeps up he's going to get sick."

"It's all of that hair," said Brutus. "It soaks up so much water he's going to look like a drowning victim soon."

And as we watched, we saw that Rufus must have been well aware of this fact, for as he set paw for the cozy little home he shared with his humans, he shook himself, and caused Ted to cry out with annoyance.

"Will you cut that out!" our neighbor bellowed aggrievedly.

But of course that was a wholly shortsighted policy of him. For if Rufus did the same thing inside the house, it would look like a devastated area after a storm had passed through, with water soaking the floor, walls and ceiling.

Rufus passed in front of our house, and as he saw the four of us sitting on the windowsill and following his every move, he gave us a loud woofle in greeting. So we meowed a greeting in return, and Ted, noticing the attention we were awarding him and his charge, even went so far as to raise his hand at us.

Neighborliness. It's an important part of life in a small town like Hampton Cove.

At that moment a lightning bolt slashed the air, and soon a crash of thunder rattled our bones.

"Yikes," said Brutus. "The storm is right over our heads!"

"It sure sounds that way," I agreed.

"Good that we're inside," said Harriet with a shiver.

"It's not going to hit us, is it, Max?" asked Dooley, not at all happy about all of this violence. "The lightning, I mean? It's not going to hit our house and burn it down, is it?"

"It won't hit the house," I assured my friend. "We're not the highest point in the area, so if it does hit something, it will hit that."

"What is the highest point in the area?" asked Harriet.

We all glanced at the lamppost in front of the house, and I wondered if that might be the highest point in the immediate vicinity of the house. And it was as I measured the lamppost with my eyes, trying to gauge its height relative to the surrounding houses, that I caught sight of something lurking on top of the thing. I could have been mistaken, of course, since it was very hard to make out, but there seemed to be some kind of bird or other creature up there.

"Do you guys see that?" I asked. "It's almost as if there's something on top of that lamppost."

"Impossible," said Brutus. "In this weather it would have to be crazy to venture outside."

"I think Max is right," said Harriet. "There is something on top of that lamppost. Though I can't make out what it is."

"Could be a bird," I ventured.

"Or a rat," Harriet offered.

"It's probably a figment of your imagination," Brutus scoffed. "Or simply a trick of the light."

"Whatever it is, it should probably get down from there," said Dooley. "Cause it's not safe."

As if to confirm his words, suddenly lightning struck

again, only this time it actually did hit a solid object in the form of that lamppost!

Fireworks exploded, and as the electricity that runs through these things reacted to this sudden attack, all the lights on the street were suddenly doused and our surroundings were plunged into darkness.

"Oh, no!" said Dooley. "That poor creature!"

"It's probably fried now," Brutus grunted.

"I'm not so sure," I said. For just before the lights went out, I thought I'd seen something being catapulted from the top of that lamppost and landing in our front yard. "I think it's right…" I pointed to a spot in front of us. "There."

And lo and behold, as we all looked, a small furry creature, illuminated by the light of the window, stood up, dusted itself off, and shook its tiny head.

"Is that…" said Dooley.

I nodded grimly. "A mouse," I said.

"And a pretty tough one, too!" said Brutus.

CHAPTER 3

*I*n spite of my earlier stated philosophy never to venture out into a raging storm—especially when your neighborhood has just suffered a massive blowout—we decided to see if that unfortunate mouse was all right. Now as a rule cats and mice don't get along all that well. But at least in our corner of the world this doesn't necessarily have to be the case. Case in point: once upon a time Harriet had been the victim of a mouse attack, and even she had never struck back at those mice in anger. To be fair, the mice had been in the majority at the time, and had even managed to momentarily render Harriet a spent force by locking her up.

Mice are cunning that way.

This mouse didn't seem to be accompanied by any relatives at all, and so we figured we were probably going to be safe.

"Poor little thing," said Dooley, who has always been a kind-hearted cat. "I hope it's going to be all right, Max."

"I hope so, too," I said. I'd heard some stories about people being struck by lightning, and even though some of them had survived, it did give them quite a shock, and a lot of them were never the same again.

We hurried out of the pet flap, located in the kitchen door, then rounded the house and arrived just in time to see the mouse looking both discombobulated and confused, which was hardly surprising.

"How are you?" I asked therefore.

"Are you hurt?" asked Dooley.

"No, actually I'm fine," said the mouse, and looked surprised.

"He's fine," said Brutus. "Let's go back inside."

"Maybe you think you're fine, but in actual fact the real impact of what happened will hit you later," said Dooley. "It's often that way. Won't you come inside for a minute? You can rest and get back on your feet."

"That's very kind of you, Dooley," said the mouse.

For a moment it didn't register, but then it did. "How do you know my name?" asked Dooley. Then his eyes widened. "Oh, no! That lightning strike has given you psychic powers! You can read my mind!"

"Don't talk nonsense, Dooley," Brutus grunted. "That kind of stuff doesn't exist, except in fairy tales and Hollywood movies." He eyed the mouse suspiciously. "What's your angle, mouse? What's your game?"

"No game," the mouse assured us. "But it's true that I have heard about you guys. But then who hasn't? You're pretty famous around these parts. Especially Max, of course, and his loyal sidekick Dooley."

"And what about me?" asked Harriet eagerly. "Have you heard about me?"

"Of course," said the mouse. "The beautiful and elegant Harriet. How could I not have heard of you? And then there's Brutus, of course. The brave and strong Brutus."

"The kid's all right," said Brutus, mollified.

I studied the mouse a little more closely, and saw that it had scorch marks on its back, and that its whiskers were burned off at the tips. But all in all it had survived that lightning bolt remarkably well.

"Must be the size," said Dooley, as if reading my mind. "The smaller the size, the easier it is for a creature to survive a lightning strike unscathed. If it had happened to you, Max, you would have been a goner for sure."

I didn't know whether to take this as a good thing or a bad thing, so I simply nodded my acknowledgment.

"Let's go inside," I suggested, for I was gradually freezing my tushy off, and if there's anything I dislike it's being cold.

The mouse didn't need to be told twice, and so it obediently followed us into the house, and parked itself near the radiator so it could warm its tiny carcass.

"You haven't told us your name," I said.

"Lucifer," said the mouse, which struck me as quite ominous.

"Maybe that's why you didn't burn," said Dooley, nodding. "With a name like that you're used to being lit up."

The mouse smiled an indulgent smile. "I didn't choose the name. My dad did. We come from a long line of mice that like to live on the edge of society, you see, where life is lived in precarious circumstances."

"So where do you live?" I asked.

"In a large factory where they used to make matches," said Lucifer, which made a lot of sense. "I don't know if you've heard of the place? It's located near the mall. It was closed down probably thirty years ago."

"Oh, that's right," I said. "The Lucifer Match Factory. Of course."

Lucifer nodded as he warmed his tiny paws against the radiator, which was giving of its best. "It's not a very nice place, I can tell you that. But since my family has lived there for generations, it's the place we call home. In fact I'm probably the twelfth-generation Lucifer in my family, which tells you something about how long we've been out there."

"So what brings you to this part of town?" I asked.

"Yeah, you're far from home, young Lucifer," said Brutus. "You must have walked for miles to get here."

"I did, actually," the little rodent confirmed. "And with only one goal in mind." He turned a pair of hopeful eyes on me. "To speak to the one and only Max, hoping he would be able to lend a listening ear and provide me with a solution for my family's most terrible predicament."

I frowned. It isn't every day that a mouse pays me a visit. "A solution for what?" I asked therefore.

The mouse paused and suddenly looked bashful. "I've climbed hills, I've crawled through sewers, I've scaled cars and traversed gardens and squares filled with every manner of menace. I've even been zapped by lightning. All this so I can ask you one question, oh great Max."

"Shoot," I said, starting to feel a little ill at ease. I'm not used to all this praise, you see. And I wasn't entirely sure what to think of it.

The mouse closed his eyes and what was left of his whiskers trembled violently as his mind shot back to whatever question he was working himself up to ask.

"My family is in awful danger, Max. That old match factory is in the process of being sold to a consortium of investors who are going to tear it down and turn it into a new development. What these investors have in mind with the property, I don't know, but what I do know is that the place where the Lucifer family has lived since the dawn of time will soon be destroyed. And so I beseech you, Max, to help us find a solution. If not..." He swallowed once or twice. "Life as we know it is over. Where are we going to live? What are we going to do? We'll all die, Max!"

"You could always move to the mall," Brutus suggested, earning himself a scathing look from the tiny mouse. "No, I mean it's a great place, with plenty of food and plenty of space where your family can live. Okay, so maybe you'll have to change your name to something other than Lucifer, but that's not such a hardship, is it? You could call yourselves… the mall rats. Though maybe not," he added belatedly.

"Or the mall mice?" Dooley suggested.

"See? Mall mice. Got a nice ring to it, wouldn't you say?"

"It's not that," said Lucifer. "It's just that… my family is very big, Brutus. There's simply no way we'd ever fit into that measly mall."

We all stared at the mouse. "So… how big is your family, exactly?" I asked finally.

"At last count?" He thought for a moment. "It's hard to know for sure, of course, since the situation keeps evolving on a daily basis. But I'd say… about twenty, maybe?"

"Twenty? That's not a lot," said Brutus with a grin.

"Twenty million, Brutus," Lucifer specified.

I think our jaws all dropped to the floor. "Twenty million mice!" Harriet cried. I noticed she'd gone a little pale beneath her fur. "But that's awful! That's just terrible!" But when Lucifer's expression darkened, she hastened to add, "I mean it's terrible that they're destroying your home!"

"It is terrible," Lucifer confirmed sadly. "Which is why I decided that I needed to find a solution and fast, too. My family doesn't believe there's anything we can do, you see. They're pretty defeatist in their outlook. But I know that the great Max must be able to come up with something. Your reputation has spread all the way to our factory, Max, and so when I heard about the amazing feats of brilliance you've worked to perform, I decided to ask for your help." He looked at me beseechingly now. "Can you do something, Max? Can you save us? Please tell me yes, you can."

"Yeah, Max," said Brutus with a grin. "Please save Lucifer's family. They're only twenty million strong, after all, and pretty soon now they'll be out of house and home."

"Oh, Max, you have to help Lucifer," said Dooley. "Think hard, Max. Use that big brain of yours, please."

The only one who hadn't said anything was Harriet, and I turned to her now, hoping she had some brilliant idea or helpful comment to make. But instead she said, "I can't even begin to imagine how much food you need to feed twenty million mice! And how much space you guys need!"

"Exactly," said Lucifer. "Which is why I think the mall isn't big enough for us. The Lucifer Match Factory is one of the biggest factories in the area, and since it was closed down has provided us with plenty of space. But now that it will be demolished, I don't know what we'll do."

"You could always come and stay with us," Dooley suggested. "I mean, it's not as big as your factory, but we do have a basement."

His comment was met with three looks of abject horror and one smile. The smile was Lucifer's, and for a moment I was afraid he was going to accept Dooley's crazy offer. But instead he said, "That's very kind of you, Dooley, but this house simply isn't big enough—even if you add in the basement." He thought for a moment. "Unless you've got a very, *very* big basement that runs underneath these streets for miles and miles?"

"Nope," said Brutus. "Just the regular-sized basement, I'm afraid."

Lucifer shook his whiskered head. "Then I'm afraid it won't do."

"Oh," said Dooley, much disappointed. "Okay, then I guess it's up to Max to come up with a solution."

Oh, boy. Talk about an impossible situation!

CHAPTER 4

It didn't take long for Sidney Grant to realize he was in a lot of trouble. Even as a kid he'd been a great trencherman, happy and eager to stuff his face with all manner of pastry and starchy foods, but it was clear he was in over his head. The burger eating contest he had entered at the instigation of his girlfriend Caroline wasn't going too well for him.

Even as he stuffed another burger into his mouth he glanced sideways at contestant number eight, and saw that he was way ahead of him. Looking to his left, contestant number three was even further along. And so he finally realized that what he had always thought of as his most appealing and prominent feature—namely his capacity to eat large quantities of food in a short amount of time—was utterly failing him.

Even as a young boy his friends in school would give him their uneaten burgers to finish off, or the leftovers from their plates, which he gladly polished off. At first he'd done it just to be liked, since eating all of his friends' leftovers and uneaten contents of their lunch boxes earned him a lot of laughs. He even remembered one time when his entire class had gathered around to see if he could actually stow away all of the food gathered on his tray. It was the contents of the school canteen, and his friends had thought it funny to raid the canteen and put it in front of him as a challenge. They'd filmed the entire scene and later put it online as a YouTube video, which had quickly gone viral and had solidified his reputation as the premier eating machine of his generation.

And now this. He was going to lose, he thought sadly as he put another burger into his mouth and chomped it down. Already he was about a dozen burgers behind contestant number three, and he'd even lost track of how many burgers contestant number eight had downed. Possibly two dozen more than him, which was simply insane.

He finished the final burger on his plate, and immediately the empty plate was yanked away and replaced by another one, filled with another dozen burgers. He eyed the plate for a moment and flinched, and that's when he knew he was done. Never flinch at one of these contests is the golden rule. If you pause for even one moment, you break your rhythm and you'll never get into the groove again. Your stomach won't let you.

So he looked to his left, then to his right, his hands on the burger but not having put it into his mouth just yet, then looked out into the audience and locked eyes with Caroline, and sadly shook his head.

He could see the look of disappointment on her face, but that couldn't be helped. He was full. No room for even a scintilla of a gram of a patty.

"You loser!" Caroline screamed. "You stupid idiot, Sidney!"

"I'm sorry, baby!" he yelled back, much to the amusement of the rest of the audience, who all cheered and clapped at this display of marital discord, even though Caroline and Sidney weren't even married.

"Don't you dare, you piece of shit!" Caroline said.

"I can't!" he cried, holding up his hands. "I'm full!"

"If you don't start eating right now I'm breaking up with you!"

More jeers and shouts. The audience was really having a ball.

Not so much Sidney, though. He had signaled to the referee that he was throwing in the towel. But as he got up from the table, suddenly he felt oddly faint. And as he went down, the whole world turned dark.

When he came to, he was feeling nauseous, and as he opened his eyes, for a moment he thought he had died and gone to heaven, for the most gorgeous redhead was looking him straight in the eyes. Before long, though, her face was supplanted by the round face of his girlfriend Caroline, who didn't look worried at all. She looked angry. Seething!

"You told me you had this, Sidney," she snapped. "You told me this was going to be a walk in the park for you! That's a year's supply of free burgers down the drain. I was really looking forward to that, you know."

"I'm sorry, baby," he said. "I guess the competition had the edge."

"I'll give you an edge!" she yelled, and abruptly smacked something wet and squishy into his face and mashed it across his brow. He stuck out his tongue and determined it was one of the burgers he had failed to eat. But when he had wiped the remnants from his eyes and looked up, he saw that Caroline had left the venue. He could see her stalking off in the distance, clearly too angry to stick around for even one minute more.

The pretty redhead was back, and now he saw she was wearing a white outfit and realized she was one of the medics hired to ensure the health and safety of both contenders and attendees of the eating contest. He briefly wondered if she had placed those luscious lips on his and given him CPR. If she had, unfortunately he couldn't remember.

"Are you all right, sir?" she asked.

"Feeling a little nauseous," he replied.

She smiled. "That'll go away. Can you sit up?"

He tried to sit up, and with her assistance he finally managed. And just as he did, suddenly he felt a powerful lurching sensation in the pit of his stomach, and presently he was throwing up all of those burgers he'd just downed, a great portion of which landed on the pretty nurse's front.

"Oops," he said finally as he wiped his lips. "I'm so sorry."

"That's all right," she said, but she didn't sound as if she was all right.

When looking back on his life later, this was the moment he would have singled out as the decisive moment. The moment when he decided to turn his life around. And so he made up his mind never to enter an eating competition ever again in his life. In fact he was done with overeating in general. The look that poor nurse had given him—a look of loathing mixed with pity—was enough to put himself in her shoes and see himself as she saw him: as an overweight, slightly ridiculous young man who was digging himself an early grave with his teeth.

"Enough," he said therefore.

"What did you say?" asked the woman.

"I said, 'I'm sorry.' I'll pay for the dry cleaning."

"Oh, that's fine," she said. "It will come off in the wash." Pity those extra pounds he'd been dragging around for years wouldn't come off quite so easily. He gave her an apologetic smile, and she returned it briefly before adding, "You really shouldn't do this to yourself, sir. It's not good for you, you know."

"I know," he said sadly. And wondered how he had got from pleasing his friends by acting like an idiot to ruining his health to try and please his girlfriend. Though by the looks of things she just might be his ex-girlfriend now.

"Let's get you cleaned up," said the medic, and escorted him to the bathroom. "Or better yet, let's get us both cleaned up," she added with a smile.

They made it as far as the bathroom before he had to throw up again. Only this time at least he didn't hit the medic who had been so instrumental in making sure he survived this debacle unscathed.

CHAPTER 5

The Marie-Louise was pulling into the harbor and Julius thought the sight of his home town was probably the best thing he'd ever seen. After having spent the past six months on his dad's sailboat, being home again was like balm to his wounded heart. Ever since his wife had told him she had fallen in love with his best friend and was leaving him, he'd been feeling lost and unmoored. The fact that she had also decided to apply for sole custody of their two boys was even worse, if possible, than the fact that in one fell swoop he had lost his wife and his best friend.

So he had asked his dad if he could borrow his boat for a couple of weeks, simply to be by himself for a while and collect his thoughts and figure out what his future was going to look like, and Dad had graciously agreed, leading Julius from being a dedicated landlubber to becoming a more or less accomplished sailor. Not that he hadn't known his way around the boat before he took off, since he'd practically grown up on the Marie-Louise. But ever since he'd reached adulthood he'd developed other interests, and hadn't set foot on the boat his dad owned and had attended to with loving care all his life.

The only person greeting him when he sailed into port was in fact his dad, who looked bronzed and taciturn as usual.

"Hey, Jules," said his old man as he assisted his son in mooring the vessel in its designated space. The Marie-Louise was a fine vessel, but those six months hadn't been kind to her, and neither had Julius, even though he had tried his darnedest to keep it in shipshape condition, simply because he knew how fond his dad was of the boat.

"She took a lot of damage," his dad determined as he studied the vessel with a critical eye. "We'll have to put her in dry dock for repairs." He frowned at his eldest son. "What did you do to her, for God's sakes?"

Julius shrugged. "Six months is a long time, Dad. You can't expect to sail a boat halfway around the world and not sustain minor damage." Though the 'halfway around the world' part wasn't necessarily true, as he had mostly stayed in the area, thinking dark thoughts about his ex.

"It's coming out of your pocket," Dad grumbled. "Just so you know."

"Happy to see you too, Dad," he said, and couldn't help but feel a sense of disappointment at the cold reception he was getting from his old man.

Dad grimaced. "I'm happy that you got back here in one piece. After that storm last night I have to admit I thought the worst."

"I'm a pretty good sailor," said Julius. "I learned from the best."

But Dad wasn't so easily placated. "Don't tell me you sailed through that storm."

"It wasn't as bad as all that," said Julius defensively.

"Are you crazy? You could have sunk the Marie-Louise!"

Or he could have been swept overboard and drowned. But apparently his dad was more concerned with the fate of his stupid boat than that of his offspring. "Have you heard from Matt?" he asked, referring to his younger brother.

"Oh he's in South America again," said his dad with a dismissive gesture. "Not sure what he's up to this time. Last time it was gold, I just hope this time it isn't narcotics."

Matt was the bad boy in the family, and had always possessed a wild streak that had brought him a lot of trouble but also a lot of crazy stories that he liked to regale his family with.

"Where is he, exactly?"

"Down south someplace," said his dad, reluctant to go into details. "He says he'll be back in time for your mother's birthday. Let's hope he's right, or there will be hell to pay this time."

Matt had missed Mom's birthday three years in a row, and Dad had told him that if he missed it again he shouldn't bother coming home at all. Then again, Dad had used threats to try and cajole Matt into submission before, but when push came to shove, Julius's kid brother always managed to make him eat his words. Charm personified, he always had been able to twist his parents around his little finger. It had led to some epic arguments between the two brothers, since Julius felt he always bore the brunt of the trouble his brother caused, while Matt simply went off on his next crazy adventure, to hell with the consequences for his family.

Ten minutes later Julius was seated next to his dad while the old man drove the family Jeep in the direction of the home that had been in the family for generations. Located on a bluff that oversaw a small bay, they affectionately called it The Chapel, since it bore a striking resemblance to this type of edifice, only bigger and more accommodating to a family.

"So have you heard from Jessica?" asked Julius finally, after they had traveled in silence for about twenty minutes.

His dad took a firmer grip on the steering wheel. "Nope," he said, his response to the touchy topic typically terse.

"Did you at least see the kids?"

But Dad shook his head.

When Jessica divorced Julius she was granted sole custody of the boys. She'd been so angry with him that she'd sworn a solemn oath he would never see them again, and apparently that also extended to his family.

"That's crazy," he said in a low voice. "She shouldn't take the beef she has with me out on you guys."

Dad sighed. "I guess that's not the way she feels, son." He glanced over at him. "So have you decided to tell your mom about what happened between you and your ex-wife?"

His jaw worked. "Not yet."

"Six months not long enough to screw up your courage?"

He shook his head. "Not by a long shot, I'm afraid."

Another sigh from his dad. "Maybe it's for the best. She'll just worry, and she hasn't been feeling so great lately."

"You want me to lie to her? Tell her everything is fine?"

"That's exactly what I want," said his dad. "You tell her exactly what she wants to hear, and then you'll get in touch with Jessica and convince her to let us see our grandkids again."

"I'm not sure that's possible, Dad. She did take out that restraining order against me, and apparently that applies to you guys as well."

His dad frowned. "That's too bad. Cause like I said, your mother hasn't been feeling well."

The way his dad said it had him look up. "You mean..."

His dad nodded. "She saw Doctor Poole last week, and even though she keeps telling me everything is fine, I have a hunch she might be lying." His hands gripped the wheel a little tighter. "I'd ask him myself, but you know what these doctors are like. It's all doctor-patient confidentiality this and privacy that…"

"But you're her husband. Isn't he supposed to tell you what's going on with your own wife?"

"Not if she won't tell me the truth herself, no."

This was even worse than he thought. Even though he'd kept in constant contact with his parents, this was a piece of news they had obviously decided to keep from him until he was back. "You should have told me," he said therefore. "I would have come back sooner."

"Your mom didn't want you to know. She felt that you needed this time to figure things out. Which is why I'm telling you: try to make things right with Jessica. I don't care what happened between the two of you, stop being a stubborn idiot and try to overcome your differences."

"But…"

"Just make it happen, Julius!" his dad bellowed.

"Okay, fine. I'll give it another shot," he said resignedly.

"Excellent," his dad growled through clenched teeth.

CHAPTER 6

*D*ooley wasn't aware of the fact that he had officially joined the Mouse Protection League, but all the talk amongst his closest friends told him this was probably the case. It was a strange situation he would have said, since historically cats aren't usually engaged to fight on the side of mice, or even being recruited by them as their greatest defenders. Quite the contrary, in fact. Cats have always been recruited by humans to help them deal with mice infestations and to keep them from destroying their crops and their harvests and such. So now they would have to organize what to him seemed to establish the largest evacuation and successful relocation in the history of mousedom. He wasn't entirely convinced this was feasible, or even desirable.

Not that he didn't like Lucifer. He did, and he was convinced that the tiny rodent was acting from the noblest instincts. What could be nobler and more admirable than looking out for one's family and risking life and limb to go in search of the town's foremost feline problem solver in a bid to save your family's lives? And so even though he was all for it, secretly Dooley harbored doubts and fears—doubt whether even Max was capable of pulling off such an incredible feat. And fear that if he and his friends got involved, they might encounter a backlash from their humans, who might not be fully on board with this rescue operation as it was being sold to them. On the contrary: their humans might put their foot down, or else they might find themselves on opposite sides of the fence, with their humans actively working against them. And if there was anything Dooley didn't want, it was to alienate his humans, something called biting the hand that feeds. It wasn't a sound survival strategy.

"How are we going to pull this off, Max?" he asked therefore.

"I have absolutely no idea," Max confessed. "So if you have any bright ideas, now is the time to offer them, buddy. How do you save twenty million mice? And when did this suddenly become our problem in the first place? In other words: why me? Why us?!"

"Because you're the cleverest cat in town," Dooley said, and he meant it, too. "Though this seems like a tall order even for you, Max. I mean, it might endanger our good relationship with our own humans, you know. Odelia might not like it when we start relocating millions of mice. You know what humans think of mice. They don't like them very much!"

"No, mice most definitely have a serious PR problem," Max agreed.

The two friends were located on the back patio, enjoying a break after the storm. Overnight the rain had finally stopped, and that morning the sun had broken through the clouds and it was as if all of nature had suddenly relaxed and decided that maybe enough was enough now.

Lucifer had returned to his family, to give them the good news that the famous cat detective Max had accepted to take

31

on their case, and now it was left to Max and his friends to come up with a plan. What plan, clearly no one knew!

"Maybe we can just forget about it?" said Dooley. "I mean, Lucifer is gone, and so maybe if we pretend that he was never here in the first place it will be all right?"

"I'm not so sure that's a good idea," said Max. "It sounds to me like the strategy of the ostrich, and we all know that's not a great way to tackle a problem. Invariably the problem returns, only this time a little tougher and harder to deal with. And besides, did Lucifer strike you as the kind of mouse you can simply ignore and he'll slink off into the background and go away?"

"Not exactly," Dooley admitted. "He struck me more like the kind of mouse who'll be all over you—in your face and screaming his little head off that you broke your promise."

"That's what I'm afraid of," said Max. "That he'll simply come back and keep coming back to badger us until we finally give in." He shook his head. "No, we gave our word, Dooley, and now we have to honor it."

It was a sad affair when the likes of Lucifer could simply barge in and start throwing their weight around, however slight. Then again, twenty million lost souls wasn't nothing. The thought of all of those mouse lives being endangered by the plans of some faceless corporation intent on destroying their home brought tears to Dooley's eyes. "Okay, so we better talk to Odelia," he said. "'Cause this is a lot bigger than the four of us, Max. And I don't think we can solve this all by ourselves."

"You're right," said Max, much to Dooley's surprise. "We need to talk to Odelia and tell her what's going on. So she can talk to Charlene, and Charlene can come up with a solution. She's the Mayor, after all, and this business with the Lucifer Match Factory sounds like something that's right up her alley. She's used to dealing with these big developers."

"They will simply destroy Lucifer's family," said Dooley moodily. "You know what these big conglomerates are like. All they care about is making a profit. They don't care about a bunch of little mice."

"That's not necessarily true," said Max. "In this case we just might have some allies on the human side. Remember that frog pond?"

Dooley threw his mind back and tried to remember a pond and frogs. He drew a blank. "Um, no," he finally admitted. In all likelihood it was some obscure story Max had read about, and being as clever as he was and always assuming everyone else was as clever as him, he figured they were fully on board every step of the way.

"There was this pond located on a piece of land that was going to be turned into a new development. A housing development if I remember correctly. So they applied for the necessary permissions, and everything was going well, until some environmentalists pointed out that some very rare species of frogs had their home in that pond, so they filed a complaint against the development of that land. According to them the frogs were an endangered species and should be protected. There were protest marches and a petition campaign and they even showed up outside Charlene's home a couple of times. In the end the town council decided not to grant permission to develop that land, and instead turned it into a nature reserve. They named it Frog Park and it's a popular tourist destination now, with respect to the frog species, of course."

"Oh, I do remember a couple of men with long beards and women with tattoos and piercings showing up on Charlene's doorstep," Dooley said, nodding. "They were shouting slogans and generally making a nuisance of themselves. I didn't know it was connected to frogs, though."

"Okay, so maybe Charlene might be induced to do the

same thing for the Lucifer family. Though I don't think we can argue that mice are an endangered species. That would probably be stretching the truth a little."

"Charlene might argue that there are too many mice in the world."

"Let's just give it our best shot," said Max finally as he clapped his friend on the back. "That's all we can do, after all."

It didn't sound particularly inspiring, but Dooley had to agree that Lucifer couldn't very well expect them to pull off the impossible. They were cats, after all, not miracle workers.

"It's going to be a challenge, Max," he said.

"And when have we ever shied away from a challenge?"

"Um… never?" he said, wondering if this was a trick question.

"Exactly! So let's just talk to Odelia and take it from there. After all, we can't do this ourselves. It's going to take a coalition of the willing."

"A coalition of what, Max?"

"Of the willing. You know, of people who are willing?"

"Willing to do what?"

"Whatever we ask them to do, basically. Or whatever Lucifer is asking us to do."

"Shouldn't we call it a coalition of Lucifer, then?"

"All right. Let's call it the Lucifer Coalition. It's got a pretty nice ring to it, don't you think?" Max was smiling, which gave Dooley hope that this might turn out all right after all.

"The Lucifer Coalition," he said, trying the peculiar phrase out for size. "It does have a nice ring to it," he agreed.

"Let's find Odelia and give her the good news."

Oh, boy. Somehow Dooley had the feeling Odelia might not agree with that particular determination.

CHAPTER 7

*J*ulius had been twisting and turning all night. He simply couldn't find sleep. And when it finally did come he had this terrifying dream where he was paralyzed and couldn't move. His arms and legs were frozen, and in fact his whole body felt as if it had been encased in amber and he'd literally been turned into a statue. He woke up drenched in sweat and flailing his arms and legs before he realized it was just a nightmare and he actually did still have possession of his limbs.

He was in his parental home, since he didn't own his own apartment anymore since the divorce. Jessica lived there with the boys now, and with Brian, of course, his former best friend.

He had his boat—or rather his dad's boat—but after having spent the past six months on the vessel he was happy to feel solid ground under his feet again and felt no need to sleep on that boat again for a while.

After he woke up and had changed into fresh pajamas— the other ones were soaked—he couldn't find sleep again, so finally he admitted defeat and got up. The night was actually pretty balmy, so he put on a sweater and took up position on the porch, gazing out across the meadows that stretched out behind the house, and up at the sky, where plenty of stars twinkled down at him, seemingly eager to convince him that there was more to life than his past and the family he'd left behind—or that had left him behind, to be more precise.

It was odd, he felt. He'd gone sailing to escape from his life, but now that he was back he realized that there was no escape possible. Maybe he simply had to tackle it. Grab it by the horns and wrestle it down. Problem was that he wasn't the wrestling kind of guy. He was more the live-and-let-live type of person. Contrary to his brother, who had always gotten into all kinds of trouble because of his do-or-die approach to life.

The screen door opened and closed and when he looked up he saw that his mom had joined him.

"Can't sleep?" she asked.

"Nope. I had a nightmare."

"About Jessica?" she asked as she took a seat next to him.

"No, I was paralyzed. Couldn't move. Like I was a fly caught in amber. It was very weird and very unpleasant."

She nodded. "You had that dream before."

"I did?"

"Oh, sure. You probably don't remember, but when you were about five or six it would be a recurring thing. You would wake up in the middle of the night screaming and kicking, your pillow and your sheet on the floor, claiming you couldn't move and you couldn't breathe. Finally we took you to see a child psychologist, who told us it wasn't an uncommon thing and we shouldn't worry too much about it. She figured it would probably go away by itself, and it did."

"So what caused it?" he asked, wondering why he didn't remember any of what his mom was telling him.

"She figured it might be connected to the death of your sister," said Mom. "She died when you were—"

"Three. Yeah, I know." He barely remembered anything about his sister, apart from the fact that one day she had gone to the hospital and had never come home again. And also that his mom and dad had been very sad for a long time —especially his dad, who was very attached to his firstborn, who was only six when she died.

"They figured that you might have suffered a trauma when Vicky died, and that this was manifesting in your feeling paralyzed—though it was only in the dream. You never actually did suffer from paralysis."

"Thank God," he said. "Imagine not being able to move all of a sudden. That must be pretty terrible."

She smiled. "Yeah, I can't imagine it's a lot of fun."

For a moment they didn't speak, but simply enjoyed each other's company and being out there in the silence of the night.

"I missed you, you know," said his mom. "I thought you were never coming back."

"Oh, I was always coming back," he said. Even though that wasn't necessarily true, of course. There had been times when he had considered never coming back at all. What had stopped him was the notion that his mom and dad were still alive, and they would suffer too much if he did die. And maybe the memory of his sister had also held him back from taking his own life. No parent should suffer such a terrible shock. "And besides," he said. "I couldn't leave you with only Matt, now could I?"

She laughed this time, and it was great to hear that sound again. His mom had always been the joyful one in their family, with his dad playing the part of the eternal grump.

"So how are you?" he asked. "I mean, really?"

"Oh, I'm fine," she said, straightening the creases from her nightgown. She had pulled a cardigan over it and was hugging herself to stay warm. "The doctor gave me a clean bill of health, and told me I'll probably outlive all of you." She smiled a tired smile, and Julius knew that she was probably lying.

"That's great to hear," he said nevertheless.

"Yeah, apparently my time hasn't come yet, which is a good thing, cause I still have so much to do, you know."

"Oh, I know," he said. His mom was a councilwoman, which kept her busy enough. But on top of that she was also the chairwoman of an environmental association dedicated to conserving local wildlife, especially birds and their habitat. Safeguarding nesting colonies, reducing the number of birds killed from window strikes and protecting bird habitats in their region kept her and her corps of volunteers very engaged indeed. As a testament to her desire to protect these feathered little friends from extinction she had even convinced Dad to turn their backyard into a sanctuary for birds, as evidenced by the many bird feeders hanging from trees and also from the porch they were sitting on.

Apart from that she was also a great proponent of preserving open spaces and local natural green infrastructure and of sending developers and builders who wished to cover every last piece of land with brick and concrete elsewhere. Fortunately for Mom, she and Charlene Butterwick, the town's mayor, were very much on the same page in that respect.

"I think you're doing a great job, Mom," said Julius.

She turned to him. "So why don't you join the fight?"

"What fight? What are you talking about?" He knew exactly what she was talking about, of course, but as always was reluctant to be dragged into his mom's pet projects. As there were, preserving the living space of the Eastern-Screech Owl. Or going to bat so they could create even more diverse nature reserves on the territory of Hampton Cove. It all seemed a little pointless to him. Not to mention a lot of work.

"I've just started a new project called Green Zone," she explained. "Its aim is to entice the people of Hampton Cove to tear up as much of their paved front gardens and drives as possible and replace them with green. It's called green stormwater management and will reduce the volume of stormwater generated by rainfall to be discharged into our waterways, instead infiltrating into the ground which will remove pollution. It will also reduce the concrete jungle we're still seeing in a lot of places."

He grimaced. "I'm sure it's a very worthwhile project, Mom..."

"Oh, you have no idea. If you consider all the small patches of concrete owned by private citizens and replace them with rain gardens and bio-retention areas, it's going to make a big difference over time."

"Uh-huh," he said, tuning out.

"And I know you would be the perfect person to run this project for us."

It was a rude awakening from his reverie and he sat up with a jerk. "Me? Run a project for you?"

"Not me personally," she said. "It's been approved by the council and a budget has been allocated. Now all we need is to put a structure in place, and a person to lead the project and get the right people involved." She arched an eyebrow at him. "Last I heard you were unemployed, correct?"

"I'm not unemployed," he insisted. "I'm simply taking a sabbatical."

"So you had your sabbatical. Time to get back in the game."

He groaned. He'd been afraid of this. His mom was such a busy person it was simply impossible to relax around her.

She believed people weren't designed to take a break. They had to stay busy all the time.

"Look, let's make a deal right now," she said, sitting up a little straighter. "If you accept to run this project for us, I promise not to die on you any time soon. How does that sound?"

It sounded like blackmail, that's what it sounded like. But he was so shocked that his mom would have acknowledged for the first time that she might actually die, that he didn't voice this thought. "You mean…"

"You heard," she said, giving him a defiant look.

He swallowed. "Would I be working closely with you?"

She nodded. "It's one of the main perks of the job," she quipped.

He grinned. "So is this a ruse to keep me from running off again?"

"Oh, of course not!" she said, but he could see the mischievous glint in her eyes and knew he'd hit the nail on the head. "I'm just offering you this job because you're the most qualified person, that's all. It's not nepotism, Julius!"

"No, I'll bet it's not." He thought for a moment. It wasn't as if he had any plans at the moment. And how long could this project take? A couple of months at the most. He could probably invest that time. And if it got him to work with Mom on a daily basis, why not? If it was true what his dad had said, he needed to spend as much time with her as he could while she was still as active as she was now. So he finally took her hand and pressed it. "I'll do it," he said.

"Oh, Julius, this is so great!" said his mom. "You won't regret it."

He already did. But he didn't tell her that, of course. Instead he said, "I'm looking forward to working with you."

"And I with you," she said warmly, and gave his hand a squeeze.

The screen door swung again and his dad walked out. "What's all this racket?" he asked, yawning and stretching. "Don't you people know that it's the middle of the night and some of us are trying to sleep?"

"I've just hired a manager for my Green Zone project," Mom said proudly. "And guess who it is, John?"

"Not Julius, cause he's not looking for a job, he told me so himself."

"Oh, but it is Julius. We shook hands on it, so it's official."

"Better get that in writing," Dad said as he directed a wink at his son. "You know he's a slippery fish."

"This time I won't let him get away so easily," said Mom, gripping her son's arm and holding on for dear life. "And if you hadn't bought that stupid boat of yours in the first place, he might not have run away!"

"He was always going to run away," said Dad as he took a seat next to his wife and oldest son. "Better he took my boat than rent some piece of junk that would have sunk at the first sign of a storm. Though he did practically wreck my Marie-Louise. You should see the state she's in."

"Oh, who cares about your stupid boat," said Mom adamantly. "And frankly I hope this time she stays wrecked."

"You don't mean that, Martha," said Dad with a pained expression. Though Julius could see it was just part of the banter the parent pair liked to engage in.

"I mean every word of it," Mom assured him.

"You're breaking my heart, woman."

"Oh, no, I'm not," she said. "Your heart is too hard to be broken. It would probably need a jackhammer to accomplish that."

"A jackhammer!" said Dad, and laughed so hard Julius thought for a moment he was going to expire.

They sat there for a while, and soon daybreak started to glow on the horizon and Julius yawned. "Think I'll try and get some more sleep," he announced. He was suddenly feeling tired again.

"Sleep?" asked his mom. "What are you talking about? You're a working man now. Better take a shower and get ready to go to work."

He stared at her in dismay. "You mean..."

"Today is your first day on the job, sonny boy," said his dad with a grin. "Welcome to your new life!"

CHAPTER 8

$\mathcal{B}$arry Spence's body might be on the mend, but his mind wasn't. After that first harrowing message the doctor had given him, it had taken his brain some time to process what had actually happened. In due course a police officer showed up and sat next to his hospital bed to go over the events as he remembered them. According to the cop, who had been friendly but firm, like most cops Barry had ever been in contact with, weather conditions had been pretty awful on the night of the accident. There had been a foul storm and the rain had come down in buckets. So visibility would have been pretty bad, and the road was wet, a thin sheet of water causing the tires to come off the road at a critical moment when Barry had navigated a particularly nasty turn. According to the cop there had been no other cars involved in the accident and no evidence that there was anyone else guilty of what had happened next. Barry's car had gone off the road and down a ramp. Barry himself had been thrown from the car through the driver's side door, which, while he had sustained very serious injuries, had actually saved his life. The car had ended up in the lake and had sunk with all passengers still inside.

The news was terrifying and the shock had caused Barry to collapse, only coming to when night had fallen again. So now he would have to live with both the guilt of what he'd done and the remnants of the accident, which probably would never fully go away again. He'd have to learn to walk again, the doctors had told him, but more than that, he would have to learn to live again—as the hospital chaplain had explained.

As he lay staring up at the ceiling that night, waiting for the pain medication to kick in, his mind suddenly flashed back to the accident, and a jumble of images and sensations flooded his brain. It was all very confusing, but one thing stood out: prior to the accident there had been a blinding light. A flash that had seemingly come out of nowhere and that had caused him to turn the steering wheel to avoid a full-on collision with whatever was causing that blinding light. Try as he might, though, he simply couldn't dig up any further details, and since the police officer had assured him there was no evidence of another vehicle being involved in the crash, he figured it was probably the work of his imagination. Or maybe the blinding light was created by his brain at the moment of impact. His mind had played tricks on him before, and so he finally chalked it up to one more wrong memory in a long line of wrong recollections. Like the notion that he'd actually said goodbye to his wife before leaving for work. Apparently that had never happened either.

After running a few more scenarios through his head, he finally fell into a deep dreamless sleep, thanks to the medication he was being fed.

* * *

CRYSTAL JAMES LOOKED DOWN at the inert figure of the wounded man and her heart bled. Not only was Barry Spence a physical wreck, but the man had lost his wife and kids in one fell swoop, and frankly she wondered how he would ever come back from that. Then again she had seen many patients who had gone through similar harrowing experiences and still managed to pick up the pieces and move on.

Having served as a nurse at Hampton Cove Hospital for the past twelve years, she had probably seen all kinds of human suffering and hardship, but for some reason Barry's fate affected her more than usual. One of her colleagues had told her it was probably because he was such a handsome man, which was obvious even in spite of the many injuries he had suffered, both to his face and body, but Krystal didn't think that was the case. Even though she was a divorced mother, she wasn't looking for romance, least of all with a patient in her ward.

No, she thought it was probably the picture of the man's wife and kids on the nightstand. Barry Spence had been so convinced they were still alive, and waiting for him at home, that he had tried to argue with the doctor and anyone else who would listen to let them know he was all right. And why hadn't they shown up at the hospital yet? Didn't they realize how worried they would be about what happened to him? It had taken the police officer who paid him a visit to finally get through to him. To make him accept the truth: that his wife and kids were dead.

Krystal had been there when Barry finally realized that what the cop was saying was true, and the pain that had crossed her patient's face had touched her heart and brought tears to her own eyes as well. So much so she had to flee the room, something that had never happened before.

If the doctor saw her he would definitely have something

to say about that, and so would the head nurse. Which is why she hurried to the bathroom and had a good cry. It was at moments like these that she realized that what they were doing at Hampton Cove Hospital was only half of the work. The other half, the emotional and mental side, was probably just as important as the physical part. They could heal bodies, but they couldn't heal the person's wounded soul. Which is why she wondered if it wouldn't be better for Barry Spence to talk to a shrink instead of the hospital chaplain. Far be it from her, though, to offer such a suggestion. And so she went about her work, trying to make Barry's life as comfortable as she could, and make sure that at least the man would walk again on his shattered leg, and be as pain-free as possible.

Which is why she was so surprised when she entered his room and saw him sitting up in bed looking both energized and very much alert.

"How are we this morning, Mr. Spence?" she asked, wondering what had affected this remarkable change in the man. She opened the curtains with a practiced swoop of her hands.

"I had the most astonishing recollection," said Barry.

"Oh?" she said, checking his chart.

"I finally remembered that the accident I was in wasn't an accident at all. That there was in fact another vehicle involved."

"Is that a fact?" she said absentmindedly.

He became even more animated. Manic, even. "The reason I drove my car off the road is because there was another car in my lane, and it was going to hit me head-on if I hadn't yanked the wheel to the right. That's why I was blinded. I was thinking that maybe it was something to do with my brain being concussed at the moment of impact. But now I'm thinking it must have been an actual light that was blinding me. And as I keep going over what happened, I can see now that it must have been the headlights of the car that was driving on the wrong side of the road. So you see?" He looked up at her with feverish eyes. "I didn't do this." He had grabbed the sleeve of her uniform. "I'm not the one who killed Allison and the kids. This person almost hitting me did. We have to find the driver of this car. He's the one who murdered my family—not me!"

Krystal had been through this routine plenty of times to know what to do. After having suffered such a terrible shock, Barry Spence wasn't thinking straight. He might even be a danger to himself and others. She offered him an encouraging smile. "I'm very sorry to hear that, Barry."

"You have to get that cop in here again," he urged, still yanking her sleeve. "He has to look into this business of the second car. No way can we let this person get away with murder. And what else can you call driving on the wrong side of the road causing carnage? Maybe he was drunk, or maybe he did it on purpose. I don't know. But whatever happened, we need to get to the bottom of this and we need to do it now!"

"Absolutely," she assured him. "Let me get the doctor for you," she suggested, and managed to extricate herself from the man's fevered grip. As she turned her back for a moment, she quickly adjusted his drip so he would be fed some more of the sedative the doctor had him eased up from. It would cause him to go to sleep. And then maybe when he woke up again he'd have forgotten all about this crazy theory of his.

"Better get that cop in here again," Barry urged. "He has to start an investigation. I'll tell him what really happened, and he'll see that it's important to find this person. They'll have to answer for what they did to me and my family."

To her satisfaction she saw that Barry's eyes were already drooping closed and that his voice was weakening.

"Take a rest," she suggested, tucking him in again. "And I'll talk to the doctor and ask him what we can do for you."

"Talk to the cop," he insisted weakly, but finally his eyes closed and his head slumped back against his pillow. His cheeks were red, she now saw, and wondered if the doctor had been too quick to wean him off those sedatives. Barry had broken his leg in three places, had a splintered kneecap and a terribly complicated ankle fracture. He would walk again, after some serious rehabilitation, but he would never be the same again.

She looked down at him and wondered what she should do. Chances were that when he woke up he'd have completely forgotten about this cockamamie story about the second car. The police had conducted an investigation and had assured Barry that he had been alone on the road that night. The accident had even made it into the paper, and there it had also clearly stated that an unfortunate accident, due to the awful weather conditions that night, had taken the lives of Allison Spence, 34 and Eric and Oliver Spence, respectively 3 and 5 years old.

"Poor Barry," Krystal murmured as she left the room. She wouldn't tell the doctor, she decided. What she would do, however, was ask the chaplain if he couldn't recommend a good psychiatrist for the man. Clearly he was in a lot of pain of a kind no painkiller could remedy.

CHAPTER 9

A mouse might be a tiny creature but that doesn't mean it can't have a big impact. I could see this impact now firsthand when Dooley and I told Odelia about our decision the night before to help out Lucifer and his family. Suffice it to say that Odelia wasn't fully on board our coalition of the willing. In fact it wasn't an exaggeration to say that she wasn't willing at all. On the contrary. She was vehemently opposed to the idea.

"Look, first you brought a rat into my home," she said, referring to a recent incident where Dooley had invited a pet rat to come and live with us, "and now you want to bring twenty million mice in here? Read my lips, Max: no way!"

Dooley, who was staring at Odelia's lips, said, "It's not easy reading your lips, Odelia. Could you repeat that, please?"

Odelia smiled at this. We were in the kitchen, where she was enjoying a nice cup of coffee, her first one of the day, which always put her in a good mood. Even our piece of news that she was to join and support the Lucifer Coalition didn't manage to put a dent in that good mood.

"Look, I understand that it must be frustrating for Lucifer's family that the factory where they've lived all their lives is going to be demolished," she said. "But you know, that's just tough luck. They'll just have to find some other place to live. And I don't see why it's any concern of mine, to be honest. As it is I have different fish to fry."

This had Dooley intrigued and he glanced up at the kitchen stove. "I like fried fish," he admitted. "Could I have a little piece, please?"

"I mean, where does this end, Max? Twenty million mice today, a billion rats tomorrow? Or how about cockroaches, huh? Imagine if a cockroach drops by the house tomorrow complaining that his family is about to be evicted and can you please form a committee to save them."

"Coalition," I murmured.

"Whatever," she said with a sweep of the hand, almost losing the jam that was on her piece of toast. "I'm not in the habit of saving mice, rats, cockroaches or other vermin and that's my final word on the matter."

"But they're very nice mice," Dooley pointed out. "You should have seen Lucifer. He risked life and limb to come here and ask for our help. He was even struck by lightning. Fell all the way from that lamppost out there to the ground and still he found the willpower to talk to us."

"Talking about that lamppost," said Odelia, glancing in the direction of the front window. "I hope they get it fixed soon. I don't feel safe with the street being covered in darkness and neither do our neighbors."

Harriet and Brutus came walking in through the pet flap, looking well-rested, well-nourished and in excellent fettle. "We had such a great time last night, you guys," Harriet announced. "After the rain stopped we decided to go out to cat choir, and you know what?"

"No, what?" I said dutifully, even though I wasn't all that interested, to be honest. Lucifer's fate was still on my mind.

"On account of the bad weather almost no other cats had shown up! We were just a dozen or so. Even Shanille had decided to sit this one out. So instead of a rehearsal we went into town and had a bite to eat."

"That's great," I murmured.

"I overdid it," Brutus confessed, rubbing his tummy, which was pretty round I had to admit. "I ate so much I practically couldn't move."

"Probably because the restaurant had to close early on account of the fact that no customers had shown up," said Harriet. "So there was plenty of grub left over for us!"

"How nice."

Chase had descended the stairs looking spiffy in jeans and a crisp white shirt. "How do I look, babe?" he asked.

"Great," said Odelia. "Oh, that's right. You've got that meeting today. Maybe you should wear a tie?"

Chase grimaced. "You know how much I hate ties. I feel like I'm choking."

"I'd still wear one if I were you. These are important people, and if you're the only one who isn't wearing a tie you'll feel very awkward."

"Yeah, I guess you're right," he said with a sigh, and bounded up the stairs again, taking them two at a time, to tie on his one and only tie—the one he kept for special occasions.

"Why does Chase have to wear a tie?" asked Dooley.

"He's meeting some important people," Odelia explained. "Along with my uncle he's been selected to join a task force to deal with cross-county drug running. Apparently a lot of drugs have been showing up in the clubbing circuit and Charlene and my uncle want to put a stop to it once and for all by catching the people involved."

"And Chase has to wear a tie to catch these people?" asked Dooley.

Odelia smiled. "Not to catch the drug smugglers. To meet with some agents of the DEA who'll help him crack down on the smugglers."

"Oh, that's right," said Harriet suddenly. "Did you get a chance to talk to Odelia about Lucifer?" She turned to our human. "We met this really cute mouse last night? And he told us this sad story about a match factory that's going to be torn down. So now—"

"Max has told me all about it," Odelia interrupted her. "And I'm not going to touch this case with a ten-foot pole."

"You don't need to touch it with a ten-feet-pole," said Dooley, laughing. "All you have to do is find a new place for Lucifer's family."

"I'm sorry," said Odelia. "But it's a no from me, I'm afraid." And with these words she followed her husband up the stairs, presumably to wake up Grace and bring her down so she could have breakfast, too.

The four of us exchanged disappointed glances.

"Without Odelia we're sunk," was Brutus's opinion.

"We can't go and find a new old factory building by ourselves," said Harriet. "Can we?"

"We could google it," Dooley suggested. "I'm sure there are plenty of old factory buildings big enough and old enough to suit a growing family of twenty million."

"And I'm sure there aren't," I said, offering the contrarian view. "Look, maybe Odelia is right. Maybe this is none of our business. I mean, I'll bet there are lots and lots of mice out there, or other creatures, who are in trouble right now. We can't possibly help them all."

"None of them have sent an emissary in the form of Lucifer through a terrible storm to ask for our help, Max,"

Harriet pointed out. "He went to a lot of trouble to get here. The least we can do is try and find a solution."

"Okay, so if Odelia won't help us out, then what can we do?" asked Brutus. "Where can we put up twenty million mice?"

We all thought for a moment, but unfortunately couldn't come up with an answer. It wasn't just that we needed to find a very large building, but also that we had to find one that wasn't located too far from the match factory. Mice are tiny, and not equipped to travel for miles.

"Let's put a pin in it," Harriet finally suggested. "And give it some thought."

Dooley looked horrified. "Oh, please don't put a pin in Lucifer! I know it looks hopeless, but we shouldn't give up before we've tried everything possible!"

"I'm not going to put a pin in Lucifer, Dooley," Harriet assured our furry friend. "I'm going to put a pin in the problem. So let's all give this some more thought, and I'm sure the solution is out there."

"Out where?" asked Dooley.

Harriet vaguely gestured to the ceiling. "Out there."

Dooley glanced up at the ceiling and the frown on his face told me he was giving this matter of the displaced family of mice serious consideration.

CHAPTER 10

*P*epita had always been the apple of Sidney's eye. What the tiny Chihuahua lacked in size she made up for in personality. Or at least in Sidney's mind she did. So when he got home from the burger-eating contest with no prize in his pocket and minus his girlfriend, he greeted the little creature with a heartfelt embrace. Pepita licked his nose and face with abandon, as if he'd been gone for weeks instead of just the one afternoon. His mom, who had been babysitting Pepita while he was gone, because he hated to leave her alone, even if it was just for a couple of hours, looked on with an irascible frown on her face.

"I don't know what you see in that stupid mutt," she said.

"How can you say that?" said Sidney. "Pepita is the loveliest creature on the face of the planet."

"Instead of wasting all of your time on that dog of yours, maybe you should start to think about raising a family instead," said his mom, who had never been a great proponent of keeping pets. According to her they were filthy and brought all kinds of diseases into the home. Even as a kid Sidney hadn't been allowed to have a pet, or even a plush animal, since his mom felt that they attracted bacteria and fungi and could only lead to illnesses. In her mind it wasn't childhood diseases that were the real danger to kids but the habit of sleeping with plush animals.

"Get rid of all those filthy plush animals," she would say, "and we'll have removed ninety-nine percent of all the childhood diseases."

It had made for a pretty solitary childhood for poor Sidney, who didn't have brothers or sisters, no pets and also no plush animals. What he did have was food, and plenty of it, since the second-most danger to kids was a lack of sustenance, according to his mom, who, contrary to what one might expect with such a life philosophy, was a very skinny woman and hardly ever touched her food.

"So how did it go?" she asked now as Sidney checked if Pepita had enough food in her bowl.

"I lost," said Sidney sadly. He didn't see the point of lying to his mom. She had ways of finding out what was going on anyway. Call it a sixth sense but invariably she could see when he was lying to her, which had caused him to adopt a policy from an early age to always tell her the truth, no matter how embarrassing it might be. "And I threw up," he added, "all over one of the medics who were on standby in case something happened to one of the contestants. Oh, and Caroline left me."

"Figures," said his mother. "I never liked that girl. You're much too good for her. Didn't I tell you that you're much too good for that girl?"

"You did, Ma," he admitted. He liked Caroline. She had spunk. But maybe his mother was right and they weren't all that well-suited. For one thing Caroline liked weepy movies, and Sidney didn't. It's hard to settle in for an evening of Netflix and chill when you can never agree on something to watch. And besides, she hadn't been very supportive of his efforts to lose weight. Case in point: even though he'd wanted to stop these speed eating contests, she had urged him to keep going, and had even convinced him he might be able to go international and become the first Olympic Eating Champion. He didn't even think such a thing existed. She probably invented it just so they could get away from his mother, who Caroline hated. A feeling, by the way, that was mutual.

"Okay, look," said his mother as she sat him down in the kitchen. "These things will happen, Sid. That's life for you. It's going to throw you a couple of curveballs from time to time. But what you want to do is simply keep going, and keep a positive attitude. You just have to focus on the right girl and then you'll finally be able to start a family and give me a couple of grandkids—preferably three or four. Or maybe five."

It was a tall order, but if his mom said it was in the cards for him, maybe it was. So he nodded. "All right, Ma. I'll keep going and maybe then I'll finally meet the girl of my dreams."

"What are you talking about? You already met the girl of your dreams. Now all you have to do is open your mouth and propose."

"Oh, Ma," he said. Ever since they had moved to Hampton Cove when Sidney was six, and his mother had made the acquaintance of one of their neighbors, and had discovered that they had a daughter who was the exact same age Sidney was, she had gotten it into her head that the meeting must have been kismet, and that one day her boy and her friend's girl would marry and have kids. The only problem was that even though Sharona was Sidney's best friend, they weren't romantically involved and weren't even interested in each other that way.

"Look, Sharona and you—it was meant to be!" his mother

said. "So why don't you stop being so stubborn and get married already?"

"Ma, Sharona and I are just good friends. We like each other, but not like that, all right?"

"I'm sure she doesn't feel the same way. I'm sure she loves you and you're just being a stubborn so-and-so as usual," she grumbled.

Just then the doorbell rang and his mom hurried to open the door. That was the problem when you lived in the apartment next to your mom. You never had a moment's peace and she kept inviting her friends over.

"It's Sharona!" his mom yelled from the hallway. "She says it's urgent!"

He walked into the living room and saw that Sharona wasn't alone but had brought her own mother along with her.

"Hey, Shar," he said, giving his friend a kiss in greeting. He became aware that their every move was being watched by the two mothers, eyeing them closely.

"He broke up with his girlfriend, Sharona," said Ma, not wasting any time. "So I told him maybe now he'll finally get his head out of his ass and propose to you!"

Sharona laughed. "I hope not, since I'm getting married to another guy, and I was hoping Sid would be my best man."

Ma's face was something to behold. Disbelief and terror wrestled for prominence as the horrible truth hit her. "You have got to be kidding!" she cried, throwing up her hands, as if this was the worst thing that could have happened to her.

"It's true," Sharona's mom said, grim-faced. "She told us last night. Some schmuck proposed and she said yes. Can you believe it? When all the while her husband-to-be was living right next door!"

"You make it sound as if I've got some fatal disease," said Sharona as she gave Sidney a conspiratorial wink.

"You have! You're going to destroy your life marrying this boy."

"He's not a boy, Ma, he's a man. And an accomplished singer, too."

"A singer!" Sharona's mom cried. "She's marrying a singer! We all know what that means. Drugs and sex and rock and roll. There will probably be a drug bust at the wedding, and they'll put us all in jail!"

"He's a crooner," Sharona pointed out. "Not exactly a punk rocker."

"Who cares! No one in their right mind marries a singer, of all people! A doctor, yes. A lawyer, fine. But a singer!"

"Sid is not a doctor," Sharona pointed out. "Or a lawyer. And you want me to marry him."

"Sid is a good boy," said Sharona's mom, pinching Sidney's cheek affectionately. "He'll make you happy. This guy?" She made a throwaway gesture of the hand. "Forget about it."

Sharona sighed. "See what I have to put up with?"

"Watch your mouth, young lady," said her mom, wagging a warning finger in her face. "You're not too old to get it washed out with soap."

"Did you ever wash out Sharona's mouth with soap?" asked Sidney, curious.

Mrs. Jordan's expression softened. "Of course not. Sharona was always a good girl. Just like you were always a good boy. Which is exactly why you should get married. You two would be so good together!"

At that moment Pepita barked her sharp bark, and Mrs. Jordan pointed at her triumphantly. "See? Even the dog agrees with me!"

Sidney very much doubted that Pepita would want him to marry Sharona, even though she liked Sharona as much if not more than he did. She probably wanted him to be happy, and to marry someone he loved. But where would he ever find such an elusive person? He could sense that Sharona was studying him closely, then hooked her arm through his and led him into the kitchen, away from their meddling mothers.

"You look sad, Sid," she told him. "Is it Caroline?"

"I didn't break up with her. She broke up with me," he said, not wanting there to be any confusion. "She didn't like that I gave up in the middle of the competition. She called me a loser and that was that."

"I never liked Caroline," Sharona confessed. "I always thought she was too hard on you. Always criticizing you and humiliating you in public. You're better off without her, Sid."

"I guess so," he said. Caroline might not have been the perfect girlfriend, but at least she was a girlfriend. Now all he had was Pepita. And Sharona, of course. In spite of himself he had to admit it stung a little that his best friend was getting married before he did. They'd always agreed that even though they would never marry each other, they would marry on the same day, and their kids would be born at the same time so they could be friends like their parents were.

"You'll find someone," Sharona assured him. "Trust me. You're such a great guy. I'm sure there's a great woman out there who deserves to be with you." She thought for a moment. "Have you tried online dating?"

He shivered. "You know I haven't."

"Yeah, I was wondering if you had changed your mind about that. I'm afraid at this point it might be the only way for you to find someone, Sid. Unless you want to date a colleague?"

Like Sharona, Sidney worked at Town Hall. All of their colleagues were a good deal older than they were, though, and also: all of them were married and the ones that weren't didn't hold a lot of appeal to him, considering they invariably reminded him of his mother.

He sighed. "Yeah, I see what you mean."

"We could always join a club," she suggested. "A dance class, maybe? Or a yoga class?" She patted his rotund belly. "Now that you won't be competing in these stupid eating contests anymore you might want to lose some of that extra weight."

He glanced down at his spare tire, which had grown to pretty sizable proportions these last couple of years. "Maybe I should lose a couple of pounds."

"Okay, you know what? If you agree to be my best man, and help me organize the wedding, I agree to help you find a girlfriend. How does that sound? And who knows—maybe if we're lucky we still might be able to pull off that double wedding the way we always said we would."

He smiled at her enthusiasm. An enthusiasm, he might add, he wasn't feeling himself. Suddenly he was overcome with emotion. "I don't deserve to have a friend like you," he said, and put his arms around Sharona and gave her a big hug which she reciprocated in kind.

At that moment both their mothers entered the kitchen and actually whooped and applauded!

"Now that's more like it!" said Sidney's mother.

"Let me take a picture," said Mrs. Jordan, taking out her phone. "So I can show it to your kids later. Mommy and daddy's first big kiss!"

"Oh, God," Sharona groaned.

"You took the words right out of my mouth," he said.

CHAPTER 11

Since Uncle Alec and Chase were both needed at the big meeting about the drug cartel that had apparently moved into town, and none of her uncle's other officers were available, it was up to Odelia to pay a visit to the hospital where a man had made a complaint and had demanded to speak to a police officer.

Which is how Dooley and I found ourselves in our human's car on our way to the hospital. I have to say I didn't think this was a judicial use of our time, since we had a big problem to solve in the form of the rehousing of twenty million mice, but Odelia was adamant. She wanted us to accompany her, and wouldn't take no for an answer.

"So who is this man?" I asked.

"No idea," said Odelia curtly.

"What has he done?" asked Dooley.

"I don't know," she responded just as curtly.

"So why does he want to see you?" I asked.

She sighed. "Look, I have absolutely no idea what this is about, all right? And frankly I'd rather not do this at all, since I have a ton of work and Dan is already hounding me and slapping me with deadlines. So let's just get this over with so we can all go back to our own stuff."

Dooley and I were quiet after this outburst, and I wondered what was eating our human that she was so irritable all of a sudden. Finally she glanced at us in her rearview mirror. "Look, I'm sorry, all right? I know I haven't been in a good mood lately, and I apologize. If you want I'll talk to Charlene about the mice. Maybe she has a solution."

I smiled a grateful smile. "That's all we're asking. For you to talk to Charlene. And if she doesn't have a solution, we'll simply tell Lucifer and that's the end of it."

"We'll still have to find a solution, Max," said Dooley. "We can't leave him hanging. Or his family."

"I know," I said. "But that's not Odelia's problem, is it? We made that promise, so we have to deal with it."

"So why are you so angry with us, Odelia?" asked Dooley, who is never one for beating about the bush. "Are you having another baby?"

Odelia laughed an incredulous laugh. "No, Dooley, I'm not. And I'm not angry with you. It's just that..." She pulled a face. "If what Chase is saying is true, and this gang has moved in, things might become very tricky for all of us here in Hampton Cove. And life might not be the same again. These people are very dangerous, after all, and so I worry, you know. I worry about my uncle, about Chase, about all of us."

"I don't think it will get to that point," I said. "Will it?"

"I don't know, Max. All I know is that Chase is worried, and so are my uncle and Charlene. So I know it's serious. And it's not going to go away. They'll have to make it go away. And frankly I don't see how, since these gangs are very persistent. Once they've got their hooks into a certain territory that they've marked for their own, they won't let go."

"Maybe we'll have to move," Dooley suggested. "Like Lucifer and his family. Find a new place to live."

Much to my surprise, Odelia didn't disagree. "You just might be right, Dooley," she said softly. "If things don't improve, we may have to move to a different part of the country. And trust me when I say it's not a decision we're taking lightly."

Dooley and I shared a look of concern. "But I don't want to move, Max," he said quietly.

"Me neither," I intimated.

But maybe Odelia was right. If there were indeed some bad people intent on taking control of our town, maybe there was no other choice than to leave at some point.

"When we find a new place to stay for Lucifer and his family," said Dooley. "Let's add room for our family, too. That way when we suddenly have to move, we'll know where to go."

It was a good suggestion, though I didn't think Odelia and her family would enjoy shacking up with a couple of million mice in some old factory. Then again, maybe it had a custodian area where we could live?

It didn't take us long to arrive at the hospital, and after Odelia had parked her car, she led us to the entrance, then up in an elevator before arriving on a long corridor with white walls, white floor and white ceiling and occupied by plenty of folks dressed in white. They seemed surprised by the presence of Odelia and her two cats, but didn't say anything, which told me they presumably didn't have an anti-pet policy like some hospitals do. Of course Dooley and I are very hygienic pets, and always make sure we're perfectly groomed and follow the most stringent hygiene procedures. In fact any hospital can probably learn a thing or two from us. Except maybe the part about licking our own butts. But then I guess nobody's perfect.

We arrived at the room in question, and when we saw the

man lying in his hospital bed I wondered again what this was all about.

He seemed to feel the same way, for when he opened his eyes and laid them on us, he frowned. "Who are you?" he asked, sounding none too friendly.

"Odelia Kingsley," said Odelia. "I work with the Hampton Cove police." She produced the badge her uncle had given her and I wondered if we should have brought our badges as well. Oh, well. It was too late for that now.

The man's expression immediately morphed into one of lively interest. "Oh, finally," he said. "I thought you would never get here. Listen, young lady."

"Odelia," said Odelia, taking out her electronic pad and pencil.

"The thing is that I was run off the road. My family was killed and I only managed to get out alive because I was thrown from the car. The policeman who was here before told me they had found no evidence of a second car involved in the accident, but I distinctly remember seeing a bright white light before I veered off the road. So you see, there must have been a second car, and it was driving on my side of the road and coming straight at me!"

"Slow down, Mr. Spence," said Odelia. "And please tell me the whole story of your accident from the beginning."

And so Mr. Spence did exactly that. It was sad to hear that his family had died in the accident, and that he was the only survivor. But when he told us about the headlights of the other car causing him to swerve in an attempt to avoid a head-on collision, Dooley and I were riveted. Especially when he said Odelia's colleague had assured him that no second car had been there.

It was all very mysterious, I have to say, and my interest was immediately piqued.

"There's one part of your story I find very odd," said Odelia.

"Only one part?" asked Mr. Spence.

"Well, everything about it is cause for concern, of course. But you said you received a visit from one of my colleagues?"

"That's right. A man. He gave me the news about my wife and kids, and said it was an unfortunate accident."

"The thing is, sir, that as far as I can tell none of my colleagues came to visit you. In fact I'm the first person to be sent here from the police department."

CHAPTER 12

"Twenty million mice!"

"That's right."

"You have got to be kidding!"

"I'm afraid not."

Dooley and I watched the exchange between our human and Charlene with an attentive eye. True to her word, Odelia had decided to grab the bull by the horns and raise the issue about the mice with Mayor Butterwick, also known as her uncle's girlfriend. And it was safe to say Charlene wasn't pleased when she heard the news. In fact it was probably not an understatement to say she was aghast, dumbfounded and even horrified.

"Do you really expect me to find a place for twenty million mice?"

"I promised Max and the others to raise the issue with you, that's all," said Odelia. "I don't expect you to do anything at this point, cause I'm not sure this is such a good idea myself."

"Well, at least you're being honest about it," said Charlene as she got up from behind her desk.

We were in her chambers, if that's the right word for a mayor's office, though I might be thinking about a judge. She walked over to the window and looked out across the square that separates Town Hall from the police station. If you squint you can even look straight into Uncle Alec's office and watch the great man at work. Many must have been the time when Charlene stood at this very window while Uncle Alec stood at his window and they shared loving looks and gestures. Or at least that's how I imagine it. Call me a romantic and you might be correct.

"Who are these ugly people, Max?" asked Dooley. He was alluding to the portraits of several fat and whiskered men hanging from the walls.

"Former mayors," I told him.

"But why are they so fat and what's with all the facial hair?"

"I guess facial hair used to be all the rage back in the day. And as far as the portliness is concerned, as a mayor you meet a lot of people, and often that involves having lunch or dinner with those people, and when you do that consistently over a long period of time it will have a disastrous effect on your waistline, which will start to expand."

"Let's hope Charlene doesn't fall into that trap," he said with a touch of concern.

Charlene turned back to face us. "Look, I can see that the optics are pretty bad on this one. If we don't do anything, the environmentalists will be up in arms. But if we rehouse this colony ordinary citizens will wonder why we're spending their tax dollars on a bunch of critters. Either way it won't look good."

"So maybe we should organize a stealth operation?" Odelia suggested. "Relocate them without telling anyone about it?"

"Enticing but very risky," said Charlene as she gave this

some thought. "The thing is that if it comes out, there will be hell to pay."

"It doesn't have to come out," said Odelia. "Not if you're not involved in an official capacity. You don't even have to know about it. Just give me the logistical support I need and I'm sure I can find a way to deal with this."

We didn't know what we were hearing. At first Odelia had told us she didn't want anything to do with this whole business of the factory and the mouse colony, and now all of a sudden she was going to take matters into her own hands and save them from certain death? Dooley and I shared a look of pleasant surprise.

"I knew she wouldn't disappoint us, Max," Dooley whispered.

"Yeah, looks like she had a change of heart," I agreed.

Charlene raised a curious eyebrow. "So you're prepared to take this matter in hand, are you?"

"I am," Odelia confirmed. "I've given the matter some more thought and I can't possibly let those poor mice perish just because some company is razing their home to the ground. I can't let that happen."

"You've got a heart of gold, Odelia," said Charlene, and the admiration that was written all over her features was genuine. "I don't know who would go to such lengths over a couple of critters." She threw up her arms. "Okay, well, I'll assign one of my people to set up a committee. Um, I don't know if you know Julius Gibson? He's the son of council-woman Martha Gibson and he just joined our workforce as of this morning and will be chairing his mother's Green Zone project." She waved a hand. "It's about something called green stormwater management, but I won't bore you with the details. I'll suggest he deals with those mice of yours first. Martha's Green Zone can wait."

"Are you sure you can trust this Julius Gibson?" asked Odelia.

"Oh, absolutely. I've known him since he was a kid. He's an absolute sweetheart and very reliable. His mother is one of my best friends. She's been going through some health issues lately that have put a burden on the whole family, but that's probably not relevant right now."

She reached over to her phone and got in touch with her assistant. Moments later she was on the horn with Councilwoman Gibson.

* * *

JULIUS WASN'T OVERLY pleased when his mom told him that on top of the new project he was supposedly handling, there was something else she wanted him to get involved with. It was a secret project so discretion was key. At first he wanted to refuse, but when she told him the Mayor had personally asked for him, he acquiesced. How can you refuse a personal invitation from the mayor of your town? Especially when she's your mother's best friend? It was an impossible situation.

And so he got up from behind the desk that had been assigned to him and went in search of the meeting room where he was going to meet Odelia Kingsley, who was apparently in charge of this secret project. He'd heard of Mrs. Kingsley, of course. Everyone in town had, since she was the principal reporter for the *Hampton Cove Gazette*, but also the niece of the chief of police, the Mayor's boyfriend.

He wandered along the halls of Town Hall until he had found meeting room 42b and knocked on the door. Immediately it was yanked open and he found himself face to face with Mrs. Kingsley herself. Behind her he could see two cats, which wasn't a big surprise, for rumor had it that the reporter never traveled anywhere without a clowder of cats in tow, which added to her mystique.

"Julius," said Mrs. Kingsley warmly, as she shook his hand. "So glad you could join us. Come in, please."

When he stepped in, he saw that two more people were present in the room. When he glanced over, they introduced themselves as Sharona Jordan and Sidney Grant. They exchanged greetings and he took a seat, very curious at this point what this could possibly be about.

Mrs. Kingsley took a seat at the head of the table and placed her hands together. "First of all I would like to ask you for your absolute discretion. Nothing that will be said here can be repeated to anyone outside of this small group." She eyed them all questioningly and wouldn't proceed until they had all promised to adhere to this request. Then she smiled and said, "I'm sure you're all wondering what this is about. First let me tell you that I appreciate your assistance. About twenty million souls will be happy that you're giving of your time at this moment. Julius, the Mayor has told me you're an ace organizer."

"She's too kind," Julius murmured.

"And you, Sidney, are a creative thinker like no one else she knows."

"Good to know," Sidney quipped.

"And you, Sharona—your heart for the animal kingdom and your compassion are widely known."

"What can I say? I love animals," said Sharona with a shrug.

"So is that what this is about?" asked Julius. "Animals?"

"Absolutely," said Odelia. "I don't know if you've heard of the Lucifer Match Factory?"

"I've heard about it," Julius confirmed.

"It's been empty for years, right?" said Sidney.

"There's a big mouse colony in that factory," said Sharona. "I've been out there with my group several times and it's huge. Possibly thousands."

"What group is this?" asked Julius.

"Oh, I run an environmental group," Sharona explained. "We're very concerned with the impact of urban development on the environment so we monitor things and if necessary try to raise awareness of certain issues."

"Uh-huh," he said, and thought the woman looked absolutely gorgeous. She had bright red hair and vivid green eyes and seemed extremely passionate about the stuff she was describing. "And this is all on a volunteer basis?"

"Absolutely," she said. "Though I'm trying to bring it into my day job, it's not easy. I have to say that Charlene is very receptive to some of my ideas, and so is your mother, actually." She smiled. "Martha is simply the best there is, but unfortunately there's a lot of resistance from the local business community."

They all turned to Mrs. Kingsley, curious to know more about the project she had recruited them for.

"Okay, so there aren't a couple of thousand mice at the old match factory but twenty million," the reporter now stated, drawing looks of astonishment from everyone present.

"Twenty million mice!" said Sharona. "Gee, they have been busy."

"The thing is that the factory has been bought by a real estate consortium and will be torn down to make space for a new development. And so the mice will have to move." She gave them a hesitant look. "The thing is that no one is particularly interested in the fate of a couple of million mice. So the most likely future they're facing is one of extinction.

Mice are not an endangered species. In fact they're not even a very popular species and are considered pests by most people."

"Present company included," said Julius with a grin. But when he saw the stony-faced reception his words received, he quickly wiped that grin from his face. "I mean, I like mice. They're cute and cuddly, right?"

"Nobody likes mice," said Sharona, her eyes blazing as she sized him up. "But they're living creatures who have rights. Or at least should have."

"So we're supposed to save the mice from extinction?" asked Sidney. "Is that what this is all about?"

"That's what this is about," said Mrs. Kingsley, finally putting her cards on the table. "Nobody wants those mice saved, but we're going to do it anyway. And since nobody likes mice we'll have to be discreet about it."

The three participants shared looks of confusion. "So is this sanctioned by the Mayor?" asked Julius.

"Absolutely. But not officially," said Mrs. Kingsley.

"But Mrs. Kingsley…" Sidney began.

"Odelia, please," said the reporter-slash-environmentalist.

"But Odelia—how do you expect us to save twenty million mice from extinction? It simply can't be done." This earned him a scathing look from Sharona.

"Of course it can be done," the red-haired fury said. "And we're going to do it, Sid. You and me." She glanced across the table. "And him," she added reluctantly.

"I'm not so sure about this," said Julius. "Where are we going to put them? And how are we going to move them? It's not as if we've got dozens of trucks at our disposal."

"That's why I got you three here," said Odelia. "We have a mission, we have a job to do, and now we simply have to find a solution to how to work it. I know it's not going to be easy," she added before they could all voice their protests, "but there's no other choice. It has to be done."

And all for a couple of stupid mice, Julius thought, but didn't say it out loud. He didn't like it when Sharona looked at him as if he was a piece of vermin himself. Now what had his mother gotten him involved in?

CHAPTER 13

I have to say I had my doubts about whether the people Charlene had picked would be able to come up with a solution for the rehousing of Lucifer's family. But Odelia seemed to think they would give it their all.

"I like Sharona," Dooley confessed. "I think she's probably the only one with her heart in the right place. Sidney didn't seem particularly interested in the whole thing, and Julius hates mice and is probably the wrong person for the job."

"I agree," I said.

We were in Odelia's office to discuss the meeting that had just taken place. Odelia didn't think the whole thing was a bust, though.

"You have to give them time," she said. "I think they'll be able to help us."

"What made you change your mind about the mice, Odelia?" I asked. "I thought you didn't want to have anything to do with them?"

"I didn't," she said. "But the more I thought about it, the more I felt it's my duty to do something. Nobody else will get involved, and if I don't do something to help them I know I'll feel bad about it later on."

"I'm glad you changed your mind," I said. "We couldn't have done this by ourselves. And also, I don't think Lucifer's family would accept our help, since they probably still consider us their mortal enemies."

"Okay, so now that we've put Operation Lucifer in motion—"

"The Lucifer Coalition," Dooley corrected her.

"Let's take a look at this other problem that's been vexing me. Who could possibly have driven Barry Spence off the road and killed his family?"

"And then paid a visit to the man in the hospital pretending to be a cop," I added.

"Do you think it was the same person who's responsible for the accident?" asked Dooley.

"It's very well possible," I said. "To see if Barry remembered something about the accident, and might be able to identify the culprit."

"So why pretend to be a cop?"

"It's the only way to get close to Barry," I explained. "Cops can get past doors that would otherwise stay closed. They simply flash their badges and the hospital staff lets them walk right in."

"I hope he didn't mean Barry any harm," said Dooley with a frown of concern. "Otherwise he may have been in terrible danger when he was facing that fake cop."

"I think we better talk to my uncle," said Odelia. "Cause if what Barry told us is true, there was a crime and this wasn't a simple accident."

It was definitely a baffling case, and I wondered if Barry's accident was exactly that: an accident, or if something even more nefarious was going on here. It didn't bear thinking about. But that was exactly our job: to think the unthinkable, which is what led me to my next question.

"So who is Barry Spence?" I asked. "What does he do, and do you think he may have been the target of an attempt on his life?"

Odelia had clearly thought of the same thing. "Barry is an engineer," she said, "who works for Motors & Rotors. They design and build helicopter engines for the military and are supposed to be the top company in the business. Barry's reputation is stellar, as he's the lead engineer and designer of the company, and is responsible for creating some of the biggest innovations in engine design in the field."

"So he's a very important person?" asked Dooley.

"He is," Odelia confirmed. "He's very important to Motors & Rotors, and also to the defense industry as a whole."

"I wonder if the accident could be connected to his work as an engineer," I said. "Though if it is, it won't be easy to find out, since these companies are typically shrouded in secrecy and confidentiality."

Dooley laughed. "Just like the Lucifer Coalition!"

"Yeah, just like the Lucifer Coalition," I said. Which suddenly gave me an idea. "We could always combine the two projects," I told Odelia.

"What do you mean?" she asked.

"Well, on the one hand we have twenty million mice to save. And on the other hand we have a helicopter design facility to investigate. So maybe we can use one to crack the other?"

Dooley said, "Maybe they could offer their factory to house Lucifer's family, Max? Wouldn't that be a great thing?"

"I don't think they'll be willing to do that," I said. "But they might not like the prospect of their factory halls being overrun with mice. Since as we all know mice have a habit of chewing through cables and gnawing on electrical circuits when they don't find anything else to eat." I raised a portentous whisker at Odelia, and when she didn't catch my drift I added, "If they refuse to play ball, we could threaten them with a mouse invasion. That should do the trick."

Odelia smiled. "I see what you mean, Max. But let's keep this as a last-resort option, shall we?"

I felt a little deflated, but she was probably right. Why shoot a mosquito with a bazooka when you can handle things in a more diplomatic way? I guess that's the savage beast in me: always ready to go in guns blazing!

* * *

AFTER ODELIA and her cats had left, for a moment silence reigned in meeting room 42b where the three members of the newly formed Lucifer Coalition—or committee—were gathered. Their mission was clear: come up with workable solutions to the problem the reporter had outlined. The only problem was that there was already discord in their midst. Clearly, Sharona thought, this Julius character was a mouse hater of the purest water. She knew why he was on the team, of course. His mother had probably used her pull to get him catapulted onto the committee. An obvious political appointment, something she hated with a passion.

"Maybe you shouldn't be on this committee, Julius," she said therefore, opting for an attack as the best defense. "You clearly hate mice, and you don't believe in the goals we're trying to achieve, so you better resign now and let Sidney and me get on with things."

"I couldn't have said it better," said Sidney as he devoured his sixth cookie and downed his fifth coffee. Not that Sharona was keeping count.

"I don't hate mice," said Julius. "I just don't see why we should get involved. It's a natural process of elimination."

When Sharona bridled, he quickly went on. "Mice have managed to survive for millions of years. So why do we have to spend time and taxpayer money to save them? I'm sure that once these demolition guys show up and start waving their wrecking balls around these mice will get the picture and skedaddle." He shrugged. "Long Island is big enough to accommodate however many mice, so let's just let this play out and I'm sure everything will be fine."

"It won't be fine," Sharona snapped. She simply couldn't believe how someone could be so ignorant. "This colony has made its home there. They've lived there for generations. When you suddenly displace them many of them won't make it. They'll simply die."

"So? It's all part of the circle of life. Even Mufasa had to die."

"He was murdered by Scar," said Sidney. "So that doesn't count."

Julius grinned. "I guess you got me there. Bad example. But it's true, isn't it? Mice serve as food for larger predators, just as smaller creatures like insects and larvae and eggs serve as food for mice. It's all part of the natural cycle, so who are we to interfere? If their time has come, so be it."

"What if I hired a demolition crew to wreck your house?" Sharona suggested. "And that of your entire family? And leave you all to die? How would you like that?"

"I wouldn't," he admitted. "But then I'm not a mouse."

"No, you're a rat," she bit.

"Ouch," Sidney said.

"Harsh," Julius determined.

"I think you better tell Odelia you're quitting the committee," said Sharona. "Clearly you don't believe in our mission statement so you don't belong in this room."

"Clearly I do, since I was asked to run this committee," said Julius.

Sharona ground her teeth for a moment, thinking up ways and means of squashing the other man like the odious bug that he was. But finally she decided to get over herself. There were more important issues at stake here, such as there were the survival of the Lucifer colony. "Okay, so we better get started on this thing," she suggested therefore. "Any ideas? Sid?"

Sidney gave her a blank look, a look she knew all too well. His mind had wandered, as it often did. She glanced down at his phone and saw he'd been googling something.

"What have we got there?" she asked, and before he could stop her had grabbed his phone from his hands.

"Hey! That's my phone!" he cried, trying to grab it back.

She deftly held it out of his reach and checked his history. All she could see was that he'd been googling a person by the name of Chloe James. "Who's Chloe James?" she asked, and was surprised to see Sid's cheeks redden.

"Nobody," he muttered nervously.

She clicked on a picture of the lady in question, as depicted on her Facebook profile, and saw she was a striking redhead, not unlike herself. She was dressed in a nurse's uniform. And then she remembered. "Is this the medic you puked on this weekend?"

He nodded. "I was going to call her to apologize. And to offer to pay for her dry cleaning. I already offered and she refused, but I feel so bad about what happened that I'm going to insist this time."

"What happened this weekend?" asked Julius.

"None of your business," Sharona snapped.

"I was competing in a burger-eating contest," said Sidney, the traitor. "I lost, but that wasn't the worst part. I got sick all over this nice woman medic who had to revive me when I passed out on stage."

"And this is that medic?" asked Julius.

Sidney nodded. "She was very nice to me."

Sharona smiled. She could already see what was going on here. Sid might not be prepared to try online dating, but he was prepared to call this medic, not because he was worried about her shirt, but because he liked her.

"You do this often, these eating competitions?" asked Julius.

Sidney shrugged. "Sometimes. But this was the last one. My girlfriend dumped me because she didn't like it when I quit last Saturday. Which is when I realized I probably shouldn't be doing this anymore."

"Your girlfriend pressured you into competing?"

"Pretty much," said Sidney.

"I'd say you're probably better off without her."

"That's what Sharona said. And also my mom. But then my mom wants me to marry Sharona, so she's not a great reference."

"Your mother wants you to marry Sharona?"

"She does. And also Sharona's mom. The two of them made a pact a long time ago, and the pact is that Sharona and I should marry and have lots and lots of babies."

Julius's grin was something to behold, and it irked Sharona to a great extent. "Look, this is all neither here nor there," she said. "We're here to tackle this mouse business, not discuss our personal lives."

"And so you're not going to marry Sharona?" asked Julius. "May I ask why?"

"Because," said Sidney with a shrug. "We're friends, but we're not in love or anything. And besides, Sharona is going to marry a rock star."

"Crooner," Sharona corrected her friend. "Not that it's any of your business," she added as an aside to Julius.

"A crooner, huh? And when is this marriage going to take place?"

"Um, I don't know, exactly," said Sid. "When is the wedding, Shar?"

"We haven't picked a date yet," said Sharona reluctantly. The fact of the matter was that Burt hadn't actually proposed to her. They had loosely talked about marriage, though, so it was only a matter of time before he did pop the question.

"She's asked me to be her best man," said Sidney proudly. "But only if I start this online dating thing?"

Julius laughed loudly now, as if it was the most hilarious thing in the world. "You guys are a hoot," he declared as he wiped tears from his eyes.

"So what about you, huh?" asked Sharona nastily.

"What about me?"

"You're so interested in our love lives but don't think I haven't noticed how you're being very coy about your own."

"I'm coy because I don't have a love life," said Julius.

"What do you mean?" asked Sidney. "You're such a handsome man, Julius. You have to have a love life."

Julius smiled. "Thanks for that. I'll keep that in mind for when I'm feeling a little low." He thought for a moment, then shrugged. "It's not a big secret. I used to be married. But my wife divorced me and married my best friend instead."

"God," said Sidney. "That must have stung."

"It did, which is why I slugged him at their wedding," said Julius with a grin.

"No, you didn't!"

"I did. Right after he said, 'I do' I knocked him out cold."

"I wish I'd been there," said Sidney.

"No, you don't," said Julius. "I still regret what I did, especially since my two boys were there, and they saw a side of their dad I wish they had never seen. Especially since I'll probably never see them again, since my ex-wife took out a restraining order against me the next day, and I lost my visitation rights—or any rights to see my kids, basically."

For a moment neither Sharona nor Sidney spoke. Then Sharona said, "I'm sorry, Julius. That must be awful."

"It is. Which is why I spent the past six months on a boat bobbing on the Atlantic trying to exorcise my demons and atone for my sins." He produced a weak smile. "But enough about me. We should probably get back to our friends the mice and figure out how we can save them."

For the next half hour, they actually worked well together, coming up with possible solutions to the mouse problem, and Sharona had to admit that Julius came up with some great ideas. Maybe he wasn't as bad as she thought he was.

CHAPTER 14

$\mathcal{W}$hen we met Barry Spence again it was in the safety of his own home. Though when we arrived he looked a little pale and helpless. He'd hired a nurse to provide him with some home care, and he was expecting her any moment.

"It feels weird to be back here," he told us as he glanced around a little sadly. He had decided to hold the conversation in the breakfast nook, and I could see pictures of his family on the fridge, and figured maybe it wasn't such a good idea for Barry to be back there so soon after the accident.

"I'm so sorry for your loss, Barry," said Odelia warmly as she placed a comforting hand on the man's arm.

"It hasn't really sunk in, you know," he said. "I just can't believe they're gone. When I woke up in the hospital I'd had this dream—this very vivid dream that the accident had actually happened when I was on my way to work late at night, because I had this important presentation to finish and it just couldn't wait. Allison told me not to go but I insisted and said I wouldn't be long. But then I got into the accident and when I woke up the dream was so vivid I thought it was real.

So when the doctor told me that Allison…" He swallowed away a lump. "When they told me that my family…" He dissolved into sobs and Odelia, feeling a little helpless, pushed a box of Kleenex in his direction. He gratefully dragged one from the dispenser. "I'm sorry. I'm just a mess, you know."

"And that's totally understandable," said Odelia, "after what you've been through. If something like that happened to me…" She glanced down at Dooley and me and gave us a weak smile. "I don't know what I would do. My family means everything to me. Without them I'd be lost."

"Which is exactly how I'm feeling right now," said Barry, blowing his nose in a Kleenex and wiping his eyes.

His left leg was in a cast, and so was his left arm, and he still had bandages all over his head so he clearly was still in a pretty bad way.

"He looks like a mummy, Max," Dooley whispered, even though of course Barry couldn't understand what he said.

"He's still very hurt," I said. Physically and emotionally, of course.

"Okay, so the reason I'm here," said Odelia, "is that I want to look into this business with the other driver a little more deeply. Now I talked to my uncle, and he told me that there are no traffic cameras on that road, but there is a traffic camera about five miles from there, in the direction of town, where you were heading, and so if we're lucky we might be able to see something. He's asked one of his officers to go over the footage, so hopefully that will yield something."

"That's great," said Barry. "I know I'm not crazy, and I know there was a second car that pretty much forced me off the road."

"So… do you think it was an accident?" asked Odelia.

He studied her for a moment. "As opposed to an attempt on my life, you mean?" When she nodded, he thought for a moment. "I'm not sure. The conditions were pretty bad that night, so it's entirely possible that this person, whoever he was, couldn't see the road because of all the rain coming down in buckets. I know I was having trouble, even though my wipers were on high speed they still had a hard time coping, so…"

"Your work at Motors & Rotors involves the design of top-secret helicopter engines for the defense industry, correct?"

"Yes, that's correct," he said with a frown. "Why? You think my work had something to do with what happened to me?"

"I don't know, Barry. I'm just trying to get a handle on this thing. Find out what happened, exactly."

"My work is very important to the company," he said slowly. "And it's true that it's of vital importance to national security, which is why I have a security clearance and I can't take my work home with me. But I never thought…" He winced and shifted his arm. "I didn't think it was dangerous. I mean, if it was, someone should have warned me."

"And no one ever did?"

He shook his head slowly. " They warned us not to talk to anyone about what we do at M & R. And of course never to divulge any designs. But they never said someone could come after us, or try to drive us off the road." He stared at Odelia. "Is that what you think happened? That one of our competitors tried to kill me?" He brought his good hand to his face and squeezed his eyes shut. "This is even worse than I thought."

"Do you have competitors who'd benefit from your death?"

"I don't think so. We have competitors, of course, but I'd like to think they wouldn't go so far as to try and kill off one of the other company's engineers. That would be… I mean, if that were true, I'm sure the FBI would be all over this thing, and so far I haven't heard a single peep."

"It could also be personal," said Odelia.

"I don't have any enemies," said Barry. "Not that I know of, anyway."

"What about your wife?"

"Allison? That would greatly surprise me." He directed a loving look at a picture of a smiling brown-haired woman stuck to the fridge with a magnet. "She was such a lovely person. So sweet and caring."

"What did she do for a living?"

"She was a school teacher, actually. Eighth graders. And a great teacher, too. Her students adored her, and so did her colleagues." He shook his head decidedly. "No, it's impossible what you're suggesting. Allison didn't have any enemies. People loved her. Everyone did, including me."

"Okay," said Odelia, offering him a comforting smile. "I'm just trying to get to the bottom of this thing, Barry."

"I know you are, but you're barking up the wrong tree."

The doorbell rang and we all looked up. "That must be Krystal," said Barry, and got up from his stool with some effort, grabbed his crutches and hobbled to the door.

"What do you think?" asked Odelia.

"I'm not sure," I said. "I think we need to dig a little deeper into Barry's background and also his wife's. She may have been a universally loved schoolteacher but that doesn't mean she didn't have any enemies."

"Everyone has a secret," Odelia said, nodding.

"Especially the people you least expect it from."

Barry joined us again and Odelia ended her brief conversation with yours truly. People think it's strange when cats talk to their humans. Don't ask me why, but it's one of those facts of life.

"Krystal, this is Odelia Kingsley," said Barry, making the

necessary introductions. "She works for the police department and is helping me figure out what happened to me. Odelia, this is Krystal James. She's my nurse."

"Didn't we meet at the hospital?" asked Odelia.

"We did," the nurse confirmed. "You have a good memory for faces."

"Krystal did such a good job with me at the hospital I decided to ask her if she wouldn't mind continuing to treat me in a private capacity," Barry explained.

Krystal shrugged. "I'd say Barry was such an exemplary patient I wanted to see his rehabilitation through to the finish line, but the financial aspect is also important to me."

"Krystal has two kids," Barry explained. "Two girls." He smiled warmly at the nurse and I had the distinct impression these two shared a lot of affection.

"Okay, so I'll leave you for now, Barry," said Odelia.

"Keep me posted, will you?" asked Barry. "And if there's anything else you need, please let me know."

"One thing might be interesting for now," said Odelia. "And that's the name of the school where Allison was teaching."

After Barry had supplied her with that information, albeit reluctantly, for he stressed that she was universally loved by all and couldn't possibly have been the target of the attack— if it was indeed an attack and not an accident—we took our leave. And as we walked out, I saw how Krystal leaned over Barry and pressed a kiss to the man's temple.

"She's very dedicated to her patients, isn't she, Max?" said Dooley.

"Oh, she's very dedicated to one patient, at least," I said. Though I very much doubted whether she provided this personal care to all of the hospital's outpatients.

CHAPTER 15

*K*rystal was glad to see Barry up and about. She hadn't expected him to take his rehabilitation so seriously. Most patients who have been through the kind of tragedy he had been through are in such a state of depression that it adversely affects their recovery. Sometimes they never fully recover at all, since they don't see the point of going on without their loved ones. But Barry seemed to have found an inner drive that propelled him forward. Part of it was finding the person he held responsible for what happened to his family, and part was the kind of person he was.

Already he had made great strides toward his recovery, and Krystal was only too glad to be of assistance. And then of course there was the fact that the man wasn't merely easy on the eyes but also very charming and very intelligent. She knew she probably shouldn't have accepted his offer to come and work for him. All her colleagues said she was crazy. But the money was good, and the personal rapport she had with Barry didn't hurt either. She figured it might help speed up his rehabilitation if he saw a friendly face every day, and not a different nurse sent from one of the home care agencies, of which there were plenty in Hampton Cove.

After she had checked his bandages and redressed the ones that needed redressing, she made him some breakfast, since he admitted he hadn't had any yet. Moments later they sat across from each other on the patio, where she admired his backyard, which was vast and perfectly maintained. "Are you going to sell the place?" she asked.

He gave her a look of surprise. "How did you know?"

"It's only natural not to want to be reminded of the moments you shared here with your family," she said.

He nodded. "It's too soon, of course. But I don't think I want to keep on living here. You're right. It holds too many memories. I mean, it feels like yesterday I was here with Allison and the boys, and now all of a sudden they're gone. I don't think it's fully sunk in yet. But when it does, I don't think I want to be here anymore. And besides, the place is too big for me anyway. We built it to raise a family, but now that I don't have a family anymore..." His voice trailed off, and she saw he was softly weeping. Her heart bled for him, and she wondered what, if anything, she could do. She knew how to mend broken bones and heal wounds, but what they hadn't taught her in nursing school was how to heal a wounded soul. So she simply placed her hand on his arm and kept it there until she felt the sobbing subside.

For a moment they simply sat there like that, and finally he placed his hand on hers, and she felt the warmth seep into her fingers and welcomed the sensation.

Her own husband had left her for another woman last year, so she wasn't unfamiliar with the feeling of loss. Raising her kids all by herself had meant sacrificing parts of the life she had enjoyed before, but she had made those sacrifices willingly and without thinking. It meant that she didn't have much of a personal life, since it now revolved mainly around the girls and her job at the hospital. In fact she hadn't dated since Brian left, and hadn't even been interested in that part of life anymore.

It wasn't until Barry had arrived on her ward that she felt the stirrings of feelings she hadn't thought still existed. And now that she was here with him, alone together and so close, her heart suddenly beat so hard she thought for sure he must become aware of the sound it made.

He glanced over and offered a grateful smile. "I'm so glad I found you," he said, and it made her choke up a little. "I mean, you took such good care of me back there, and now again. I don't know what I would have done without you."

"You just make sure you get back on your feet," she said, her voice a little wobbly. "So what was Odelia Kingsley doing here?" she asked, deciding to change the subject lest he figure out how she truly felt about him.

"Like I said, she's trying to find out what happened to me and to my family. She seems to think…" He hesitated, and clearly wondered how much to tell her.

"Yes?"

"She wonders—and I agree—whether what happened was an accident or… something more intentional."

At first she didn't understand what he meant by that. "Intentional?" But then she got it. "Oh, you mean…"

He nodded. "My work at the company is classified. And of great importance to the defense industry, our main client. So it's entirely possible that whoever forced me off the road had every intention of killing me. And if I hadn't been thrown from the car, they would have succeeded."

When Barry had started raving at the hospital about a second car, Krystal thought he was simply delusional, which was understandable in his condition. But now she was wondering if maybe he was right, and there had indeed been a second car on the road that night.

"But that police officer who paid you a visit..."

"That's exactly it," he said, his expression grim now. "Odelia told me she asked her uncle about it. He's chief of police. And he told her there never was a police officer who visited me in the hospital."

"So... who was that man?"

"That's what I would like to know."

Instinctively she sat up a little straighter and glanced behind her. Barry must have noticed, for he assured her, "You're safe here, Krystal. I've got security up the wazoo. And besides, they won't come after me now. Not after the stunt they pulled on the road—if that was deliberate, of course. It could have been an accident, and the man who pretended to be a cop could actually have been the driver of the car, wanting to make sure I couldn't identify him."

"But you can identify him now, can't you? We all can."

"You're right," he said, as if he hadn't thought of that before. He directed a grim look at Krystal. "Maybe you should watch your back from now on. As long as we don't know what's going on, I guess none of us are safe."

She swallowed. Meeting Barry Spence was starting to affect her in ways she hadn't expected—both in a good sense but also a bad one!

CHAPTER 16

*M*artha Gibson wondered how her son had fared in his first big meeting. She knew it probably wasn't what Julius had in mind when she had told him about working at Town Hall. But it was a job, and would provide him with some structure in his life, which she felt was exactly what he needed right now. His life had effectively gone off the rails when Allison had left and taken the kids, and she hoped he would find his feet again. Being out there on that boat had been a terrible idea, or at least that's how she felt about it at first.

John thought it was necessary for Julius to create some distance from his life and from the dramatic events that had unfolded after his marriage had collapsed. And maybe he was right. But now it was time to get back on his feet again and to face the real world, not stare at the sky or the ocean all day. Nothing good could come from running away from your problems. When you got back the problems were still there, and you had lost a lot of time—time you were never getting back.

She hadn't been keenly aware of the importance and the

value of time, but she was now. Especially after her visit to Doctor Poole last month. It wasn't too much to say she put a genuine premium on time, and hoped to use the time she still had left to make sure the people around her were happy and moving on with their lives.

She had already passed the meeting room where the meeting was held three times, hoping to run into Julius, and the fourth time she got lucky. Just as she passed, the door opened and Sharona and Sidney walked out, followed by Julius.

"Oh, hey, Mom," he said, surprised to see her, even though he shouldn't have been, since she worked there.

"So how was the meeting?" she asked.

"Oh, all right," he said, without much enthusiasm. "You know what the meeting was about?" he asked. And when she nodded, he grinned. "Of course you do. You probably know everything that goes on in this place."

"Not everything," she said. "But a lot, yes. So did you come up with a plan?"

"Not yet. I mean, Odelia Kingsley seems to expect us to find a building that will house twenty million mice. But where are we going to find a place like that? It's impossible. So instead we're trying to come up with an alternative solution."

"That's great," she said, well pleased to see him exercising his brain again. "I'm sorry it's not the project I promised," she said ruefully.

"Oh, that's all right," he said. "This is probably way more interesting than trying to convince people to tear up their front yards and plant some trees, right?"

"You're not off the hook yet," she warned him. "That project is next."

"Oh, I know," he said, giving her a peck on the cheek.

"And I'll bet you've got about a dozen projects lined up for me after that, right? Anything to keep me busy."

"To keep you moving forward," she corrected him.

"Sure, Mom. Whatever you say." He then glanced past her and said, "I'm sorry, but I gotta run. I've arranged to meet Sharona for lunch. We're going to talk some more about the project."

"You and Sharona?"

"Yeah, why? What's wrong with her?"

"Nothing. I just figured she and Sidney…"

"Mom! It's nothing like that. We're just colleagues trying to crack this very baffling problem. It's all work, no romance, I can assure you."

"Well, good for you," she said, and watched him hurry off so he could have his lunch with Sharona. She smiled. Maybe this idea to put Julius on the same committee with Sharona and Sidney hadn't been such a bad move after all.

* * *

SIDNEY HAD BEEN NERVOUSLY PACING the floor of the office he shared with Sharona and half a dozen other colleagues for the past ten minutes trying to decide whether to make this call or not. The office was empty, and he just wished that Sharona was there right now. She would have given him the final push. But Sharona was out lunching with Julius Gibson, of all people. The mouse hater and the mouse lover enjoying lunch together. Probably wanting to talk some more about their lack of agreement on this most important topic, he wagered.

And just as he thought about mice, suddenly he thought he actually saw one, its tiny head popping out of a waste-paper basket. But when he squeezed his eyes closed and then opened them again, it was gone.

God, he had mice on his mind, didn't he?

Finally he couldn't hold off anymore. So he gathered all of his courage and pressed the Call button on his phone, pressed the device to his ear and waited nervously. Suddenly a melodious voice answered.

"Chloe James."

"Oh, hi," he said. "My name is Sidney Grant. I don't know if you remember, but I accidentally threw up all over you last Saturday at the eating contest."

"Of course I remember," said the girl. "How could I forget? So how are you feeling now, Sidney? Better?"

He was gratified to know she remembered him, and was even asking how he felt. The warm feeling spread through his chest like a balm. "Oh, I'm fine," he said. "Once I got that out of my system I was okay."

"That's so great to hear. I wanted to call and ask, but since I didn't have your number... How did you get my number, by the way?"

"I called your supervisor, whose name I got from the organizer of that competition. I told him I owed you some money, so... Which brings me to the reason for this call. I really meant what I said. I want to pay for the dry cleaning. I ruined your shirt, and probably your Saturday, so if you can send me the bill I'll be more than happy to pay."

"Oh, there's really no need, Sidney."

"No, but I insist. I felt so bad afterward, so it's the least I can do."

"That's very sweet of you. And by the way, you didn't ruin my Saturday. If anything you livened it up considerably. These events can get pretty boring, you know. And anyway, I wasn't feeling like myself."

"Why? I mean, if it's not too personal."

"It's fine. My boyfriend and I broke up. Not that it matters, but it wasn't a fun experience."

"Oh, that's such a coincidence," said Sidney.

"I know," she laughed. "Your girlfriend broke up with you because you dropped out of the competition. I remember. Well, I think everyone who was there probably remembers. She was very vocal about it."

His cheeks colored at the recollection. "Yeah, she didn't hide the fact that she hates my guts," he said in a low voice.

Chloe laughed again. "I'm sorry for laughing. I guess it's human to feel a sense of relief when you see that others are having an even worse time than you are having."

"I'm glad to have been of service," he said.

"Oh, I'm so sorry, Sidney. That was such a mean thing to say."

"No, it's fine. I was just kidding. And I'm sorry about your boyfriend."

"He was a jerk anyway. Let's just say it was time for me to move on. But why am I telling you this? You probably don't even want to know."

"Oh, but I do want to know," he said. In fact he wanted to know everything about her. Everything there was to know. "So um… how are we doing this? Do I give you my address? Or maybe my email or something? You can scan the receipt and I'll pay you back."

"Or we could meet up," she suggested. "You know, maybe grab a coffee or something."

He gulped once or twice. "I would like that very much," he said finally, when he trusted his voice again. Very, *very* much.

And so it was arranged. They would meet for a coffee, so she could tell him all about her ruined shirt, and he could tell her all about his habit of throwing up on innocent bystanders. He knew it was going to be epic when he suddenly felt a lurching sensation in the pit of his stomach. Odd, he thought. Chloe seemed to have a powerful effect on him!

* * *

CHLOE PRESSED Disconnect and thought for a moment about the conversation she'd just had. It had been a nice surprise to hear from Sidney again. She had liked him from the moment he had thrown up all over her. Or maybe it would be more correct to say she had liked him from the moment his girl-friend had very publicly and very loudly humiliated him. The expression on his face had endeared him to her. And then of course he'd thrown up on her.

She hadn't thought she'd hear from him again, but now that she had she was actually glad. And she was even more glad that she would be seeing him again. She had vowed never to date again, after the way Josh had treated her, but having coffee with a total stranger wasn't dating. It was more like after-care in her capacity as a nurse. Making sure Sidney was all right.

Okay, so who was she kidding? She liked the guy. At least he didn't come across as a total jerk. In that respect he was completely different from most of the guys she'd dated these past couple of years. So much so she had promised herself she would start looking past appearances from now on, and stop dating handsome guys. In her experience they all turned out to be psychos. Sidney wasn't handsome. Not that he was ugly, but he definitely wasn't a model. So maybe he wouldn't prove to be a jerk.

She thought about calling her sister, but figured there wasn't much to tell. So instead she put her phone in her pocket and went about her business of looking after the patients in her ward. The head nurse might frown upon taking personal calls during working hours, but Nurse Ratched, as Chloe's colleagues called her, was on her lunch break, so she was in the clear.

"Excuse me," said a young woman.

Chloe turned and saw that the woman was accompanied by two cats for some reason and smiled.

"Yes?"

"I'm sorry, but who do I need to talk to to look at some of the hospital CCTV footage?"

"Who's asking?"

The woman smiled an engaging smile and produced a police badge. "Odelia Kingsley. Civilian consultant with the Hampton Cove police department."

CHAPTER 17

"Okay, so why do you hate mice so much?" asked Sharona before taking a big bite from her cucumber salad sandwich.

"But I don't hate mice!" said Julius as he threw up his hands.

Sharona grinned. Julius looked cute when he got upset. She had no idea why she was having lunch with the guy, though. She was engaged to be married, and the rules that governed human relationships probably state you shouldn't have lunch with anyone other than your future spouse. Okay, so technically she wasn't engaged, but it was only a matter of time.

"So if you don't hate mice, why do you make a face every time the word mouse is mentioned?"

"What face?" he said with a grimace.

"That face!" she said triumphantly. "That exact face you're pulling right now!"

"I'm not pulling any face. This is my regular face, the way my face always looks."

"No, it's not. You made a face when I said the word mouse."

He grimaced again. "You mean this face?"

"Oh, you're pulling my leg, aren't you, mouse hater?"

"I'm not a mouse hater! I love Disney World. In fact I used to go there all the time with…" This time he made another face, but it wasn't as funny as before. "… my kids," he finished the sentence, and bit into his sandwich.

"That must be tough," she said. "Not seeing your kids, I mean."

"Yeah, it's the worst part. And also knowing they're probably growing up hating their dad."

"I'm sure they don't hate you," she said.

"I'm sure they do. Brian will make sure of that."

"Is that your wife's new husband? Your ex-best friend?"

"Yeah, the four of us used to be so close, you know. Me and Jessica, and Brian and his wife Krystal."

"So what happened?"

He sighed. "What happened is that we all went on holiday together in the Maldives. And when we came back Brian and Krystal weren't a couple anymore, and neither were me and Jessica."

"Because… you all had a big fight or something?"

"Because Krystal and I found Brian and Jessica in bed together."

"Tough," said Sharona, who couldn't imagine going through such a terrible ordeal. "So what happened to Krystal?"

"We're still in touch," said Julius. "She seems to be doing fine."

"Did they have kids?"

"Two girls. I'm their godfather, just like Brian was for the boys."

"And now he's their real father," said Sharona, but immediately regretted her words when she saw the look of pain cross Julius's face. "I mean not their real father," she corrected herself. "You'll always be their real dad, of course."

"If they even remember me," he said somberly.

"Oh, I'm sure they do," she said. "And I'm sure if you got in touch with your ex-wife she might allow you to see them again."

But he shook his head. "Not after what happened at the wedding. She made it very clear she never wanted to see me again, and she got the judge to agree with her."

"Okay, so maybe she doesn't want to see you again, but she can't take your kids away from their father. That's just wrong."

"Tell that to the judge," said Julius, putting down his half-eaten sandwich.

"You could try to appeal the verdict."

"Oh, trust me, I've tried. But it's no good. And besides, Jessica is a lawyer, and so is Brian, so they both know the ins and outs of the legal system a lot better than I do."

"What is your profession, exactly?" she asked. She couldn't remember ever having seen him at Town Hall before.

"I'm a pharmacist, actually," he said. "Though after what happened last year I sold my pharmacy and borrowed my dad's boat and spent the past six months thinking about my life and gazing up at the sky."

"Sounds pretty boring," she said, causing him to look up at her, then bark a surprised laugh.

"You just say whatever passes through your mind, don't you?" he said.

She shrugged. "Some people find it refreshing."

"Oh, it's refreshing, all right." He studied her for a moment. "Yeah, it was pretty boring, actually. I was hoping to get some clarity, but oddly enough I got nothing. And then I heard my mom was sick, so I came back."

"Your mom is sick?"

He nodded. "Don't tell anyone I said that. She doesn't like people to know."

"That bad, huh?"

He nodded again, and she felt for the guy. First his wife cheated on him with his best friend, then took his kids away, then he lost his business and now his mom. Seemed to her the universe had decided to take a great big dump on his life. And in spite of everything he was still standing.

"Okay, so about those mice," she said, causing him to laugh again.

"Here's an idea," he said. "Why don't we simply ask all the residents of Hampton Cove to adopt a couple of mice? Let's say we divide the number of mice by the number of residents, and then we allocate that number to each household? How hard can it be?"

"And what if they say 'What? Are you nuts?!!!'"

"We leave them no choice. We tell them it's their duty as residents to adopt a certain number of mice and that's it. They don't like it, too bad."

"I very much doubt whether the Mayor will agree with that," she said with a smile. "I don't know if you know this, but politicians like to be reelected from time to time, and a policy like this will make sure Charlene Butterwick will never run for mayor in this town again."

"Too bad," he said. "I thought it was a great plan."

"It is a great plan, but not very realistic."

"Okay, so you got a better idea?"

"I have, actually. We find a different abandoned building, and relocate the entire colony. And as it happens I've got just the right one in mind."

"You do, huh? Of course you do."

They shared a warm smile, before Sharona remembered she was almost engaged to be married to her crooner, and cast down her eyes. Which is when she saw an actual mouse. Or at least she thought she did. It was giving her an intent look, hiding inside a nearby planter. But when she closed her eyes and opened them again, the tiny thing was gone.

She saw it as a sign that they were on the right track. So she took another big bite from her sandwich, and she and Julius spent the rest of their lunch hour discussing ways and means of convincing the owners of that derelict structure she had in mind to open their doors to twenty million mice. How hard could it be? Especially since the owners were the Ministry of Defense and the structure was an out-of-use military base.

CHAPTER 18

One aspect of being a cat that's not very pleasant, and which humans never take into consideration, is that our paws are fairly short and as a consequence our field of vision is limited. So when Odelia was looking at the footage of the fateful day Barry Spence was being visited by that fake cop, it was hard for Dooley and me to see what she saw, exactly. Because we were on the floor and she was on a chair sitting next to the guy in charge of security at the hospital.

"What are you looking for, exactly?" asked the guy now. He was dressed in the typical uniform of a security guard and looked as old as Gran, which is pretty old, even though she wouldn't like it when you said it.

"A cop came to pay a visit to one of the patients," Odelia explained. "Only he wasn't a cop. And so now we're very interested to know who he might have been."

"A lot of people look like cops," said the guy. "Could have been a security guard like me, or even a mailman."

"No, he said he was a cop, and he had a badge."

The guard frowned, causing his wrinkled face to scrunch up even more. "So what did he do that for?"

"No idea. We would like to find him and ask." The footage rolled on, and suddenly Odelia called out, "There! Can you pause and rewind?"

"Now will you look at that?" said the guard.

"Do you recognize him?"

"I sure do. That's Silvester. He used to work for the same company I used to work for. This was a long time ago, mind you. Before I applied for a job here at the hospital. Way better hours and better pay, you see."

"What company did you work for?" asked Odelia as she took out her notepad.

"Marginal Security. And that man's name is Silvester Muster. He has aged a bit, of course, but then I suppose I have, too. But I recognized him immediately. He always had this very specific way he moved his body. A swagger. He even told me he practiced it in front of the mirror. Figured it scared off the bad guys." He laughed. "All it did was scare off the mice!"

"The mice?"

"One of Marginal Security's clients is the Department of Defense. And more particularly their military base."

"But isn't that abandoned?"

"Oh, it is. But that doesn't mean they want any Tom, Dick and Harry to traipse all over the place. They're very particular about security. Though the only activity I ever saw was mice, and plenty of them, too!"

"Thanks, Harold," said Odelia, and I could see that her eyes were shining with excitement. "You've been a big help."

"Oh, any time. Once upon a time I wanted to be a cop myself, you know. But unfortunately I never passed the exam. And now I'm too old to try." He chuckled amusedly. "Anyway, I've got a good thing going here, so I'm not complaining and neither is my wife. Like I said, great hours and a great paycheck. What more does a person need?"

"He sure seems like a nice guy, Max," said Dooley. "So why did he let that fake cop pass security?"

"It's hard to know whether a cop is real or fake, Dooley," I said.

"But he knows the guy! He said so himself."

"I'm sure Harold isn't the only security guard around here," I said. "They probably work in shifts. So he probably wasn't even on duty when this Silvester showed up."

But Dooley's question was a valid one, and it must have occurred to Odelia, for she turned at the door and asked, "You didn't happen to see your ex-colleague that day, did you, Harold?"

"I sure didn't," said the aged guard. "And if I had I would have jumped to say hi. We had such good times together I would have loved the chance to reminisce." He chuckled again. "Like that time he took potshots at a family of mice and missed!"

Dooley frowned at the man. "I don't think I like Silvester, Max."

"No, he doesn't sound like a pleasant character," I agreed.

"So do you have any idea who he works for now?" asked Odelia.

"My best guess is that he still works for Marginal Security. He always was a career man and adamant about rising to the top."

"What constitutes the top at a company like Marginal Security?"

"Oh, supervisor, of course. Pretty cushy job if you can get it. Too macho for my taste, though." The corners of his mouth went down. "Strange mentality when you manage to rise as high as actual management. Plenty of nonsense being told."

"Nonsense?"

"Oh, you know. The usual bullshit. About launching a new civil war. Upsetting the balance of society. Weird shit."

"And did Silvester enjoy that kind of talk?"

"Not when I was around. But a guy as ambitious as him? I'm sure he adapted pretty well. Anything to stand out and be picked for lower or even upper management." He shrugged. "What can I say? It was that kind of outfit."

As we left the hospital, we caught a glimpse of the nurse who had led us to Harold. She was chatting with Krystal, who must have finished her shift at Barry's place. It struck me how alike both women looked, but then they were dressed the same, of course. When Krystal caught sight of us she waved and Odelia waved back, then walked over to talk to her.

"So how is Barry?" asked Odelia.

"Oh, he'll be fine," said the nurse. "He's a strong man with a strong personality. A lot of people in his position would simply give up and surrender to the depression, but not him. He seems determined to get better, which is all that matters."

"You like him, don't you, Krystal?" asked Odelia, who's never shy to get personal with people. I guess it must be the reporter in her.

The nurse blushed. "I don't know what you mean."

Odelia smiled. "I've seen the way you look at him. And I don't blame you. Barry Spence is a good-looking guy."

Krystal studied Odelia for a moment, trying to determine whether she could trust her or not. Finally she said, "He recently lost his wife and kids, so I don't expect anything from him. But it's true that I admire him. He's very courageous." She frowned. "He also told me that he thinks there may have been a second car on the road that night. Even..." She hesitated and lowered her voice. "Even a possibility that he was targeted because of the work he does? Is that what you think, Mrs. Kingsley?"

"Odelia, please. And at this moment I'm not sure what to think. But it's definitely possible there was a second car. And of course the work Barry does is very important but also liable to attract a lot of attention."

"Do you think he's safe out there on his own?"

"He assured me the house is secure," said Odelia. "And he has a safe room."

"He's not very mobile," said Krystal, who had brought a worried hand to her face. "If someone shows up at his door, he won't be able to run. By the time he gets to his safe room it may already be too late."

"So what do you suggest?"

"I'm not sure, but…" She thought for a moment. "He told me this morning that he's thinking about moving. Everything in that house reminds him of his family. So maybe I could suggest that he move in with me and the kids for the time being? These bad people—if there are bad people—they won't know who I am, right?"

"It's doubtful that you're on their radar," Odelia agreed. "If there are bad people, as you call them," she quickly added.

"Okay, so maybe that's what I'll suggest," said Krystal. "It's just that I'm not easy in my mind as long as Barry is out there all by himself, especially at night."

Odelia studied her for a moment. "Don't tell me you do this for all of your patients?"

Krystal smiled. "No, I don't."

The other nurse had joined us, and introduced herself as Chloe James, Krystal's younger sister.

"See?" said Dooley. "I knew they were sisters!"

"What's going on?" asked Chloe.

"It's Barry," her sister said. "Looks like he's in trouble."

"Oh, your private patient? What kind of trouble?"

"All right if I tell you later?" She glanced at her watch. "I need to make an urgent call." And with these words she took out her phone and was off.

"Make sure Ratched doesn't see you!" Chloe called out after her.

"Who's Ratched?" asked Odelia.

Chloe grinned. "The head nurse. But please don't tell her. Nobody has ever told that to her face and survived. Just kidding. She's formidable."

"I can imagine she is," said Odelia with a smile.

"So what's going on with Barry and Krystal? It's just that she's suddenly got me worried."

And so Odelia told her in a few words what was going on, neglecting those telling details that were too sensitive.

Chloe made a face. "Oh, I do hope she won't get in trouble for helping that poor man."

"She has a big heart, your sister," said Odelia.

"I know, and it's been trampled on plenty."

"What do you mean?"

"Hasn't she told you? Her husband left her for another woman last year. A good friend of hers, too. The two couples had known each other for years, and went on holiday together all the time. Until Krystal and her friend's husband walked in on their respective spouses one afternoon, in bed together. Turns out they were having an affair. They're married now, Krystal's ex and this other woman."

"Oh, dear," said Odelia. "That's terrible."

"It was. And who got to pick up the pieces?" She pointed to herself. "But she's fine now. It took a while but she's in a good place right now. Which is why I'm afraid that her getting involved with this guy Barry might not be such a good idea for her. But then that's Krystal for you. Even as a kid she would bring home stray animals. Any sick animals she'd find she would bring home with her and try and nurse back to health. It drove our parents crazy."

"Did she bring home mice?" asked Dooley.

"Birds, mice… even a cricket once," said Chloe with a smile at the recollection. "And then we'd try and heal them. It's probably where we got the nursing bug."

"I like Krystal, Max," said Dooley. "She's got her heart in the right place."

"She sure does," I said.

Krystal had returned and looked excited. "He'll do it," she said. "He'll get a cab and drive over to my place right now." She directed a pleading look at her sister.

"All right," said Chloe, correctly interpreting this look. "I'll cover for you. Just go and meet your prince charming."

"He's not my prince charming," said Krystal, stiffening. "He's my patient."

"Whatever you say," said Chloe with a grin.

We watched as Krystal took off in a hurry.

"I just hope her heart doesn't get smushed again," said her sister fervently.

Frankly speaking it wasn't Krystal's heart I was worried about. It was the people possibly trying to kill Barry. And when I looked up at Odelia, I could tell from the look on her face that she shared the same concern.

CHAPTER 19

arry actually felt excited after Krystal's phone call. He knew she was right and that staying at the house was probably not a good idea. There was the threat that was still hanging over his head, and also, there were too many memories connected to the house. Memories of his family and of the life they had lived there. Truth be told lately he and Allison hadn't gotten along all that great. She had often accused him of burying himself in his work while leaving the rest of the family stuff to her. She also told him that his kids were growing up without a father, and that time was fleeting and if he didn't take advantage of being a father now at some point they would grow up and it would be too late. Well, it was too late now, though things hadn't gone how he had expected them to go.

He always figured he had time. If only he got his career on track and got this next project off to a good start, he could relax and spend more time with his family. And now it was too late. Allison had been right all along. He'd run out of time.

He quickly threw some of his things into a suitcase,

which was hard to accomplish since he only had one arm that was functional and one leg, but somehow he still managed.

Seated on the bed he then glanced around while he waited for the cab to arrive. It almost felt to him as if he was saying goodbye to his old life and to his family. A tear came to his eye as he remembered the good times they'd had together, but also the bad. He and Allison had exchanged some harsh words from time to time and their fights had been epic. It all seemed so pointless now, so irrelevant. And if he could, he would have liked to talk to her one last time. To apologize and to tell her she was the best woman he had ever met and that life without her was going to be so rough. And then his boys. The thought of them just sliced right through his aching heart. If only he could hold them one more time...

The doorbell rang and he got up with some effort, then, leaning on his crutches, managed to hobble down the stairs. The cab driver was waiting patiently on the doorstep. He opened the door and instructed the guy to bring his suitcase down, since he couldn't possibly do it himself. Then he was helped into the cab and soon they were on their way. He'd sell the house, he thought. There was simply no point in keeping it since he didn't want to live there anymore.

The cab took off and about a minute later another car arrived and parked in front of the house. A man got out and walked around the back, brazenly looking in through the windows, checking to see if the place was deserted or not. When he decided that it was, he frowned and wondered where Barry Spence could be holed up.

Then he got back into his car and gave his superiors a sit rep of the situation. They weren't pleased with him. And that was putting it mildly.

* * *

ODELIA'S next port of call was the school where Allison Spence had been a teacher. As usual Dooley and I rode in the back of her pickup as she navigated the streets of Hampton Cove. It didn't take her long to arrive at her destination, but that time was enough for Dooley to develop an alternative solution for Lucifer's problem.

"As I see it the problem is space, right?" said my friend.

"I suppose," I said, still thinking about Krystal and Barry and wondering if they were safe.

"So guess where they've got a lot of space, Max?"

"I have no idea, Dooley," I confessed.

"In space! There's plenty of space in space!"

"Okay."

"So what if we relocate the mice to one of those space stations that float around the earth? Or maybe we could even send them to the moon on the next mission? Or Mars! Lucifer and his family could repopulate the Moon or Mars or any planet for that matter. They could be the first space colonists. Now wouldn't that be great? There's plenty of space on the Moon, Max, and also on Mars. Or in one of those space stations. What is it called again? Um…"

"The International Space Station?" I suggested.

"Exactly! I'm sure they've got plenty of room for a couple of mice, and they'd be more than happy to supply it. So we could outfit all of our mouse friends with space suits and send them off on their mission. It's going to be one small step for Lucifer but a giant step for all mousekind."

"It's an idea," I admitted. Though not a very practical one, probably. For one thing, who was going to produce twenty million space suits? And for another, I didn't think the astronauts who lived on the International Space Station would welcome the arrival of a couple of million mice. And also: what were they going to eat in space? Mice feed on bugs and such, and as far as I could tell there aren't any bugs on a space station. Or on the Moon or Mars.

But Dooley was so happy with his idea that I didn't have the heart to trample all over it with my arguments. So instead I merely smiled and said, "Sounds like a great plan, Dooley. You should suggest it to Lucifer next time we see him."

"I'll do just that!" said Dooley, very excited about his contribution.

We arrived at the school and we all got out of the vehicle. But before we could enter Odelia turned to us and said, "Maybe this is not such a good idea after all."

"What isn't?" I asked.

"Taking you guys in there. I don't think cats are allowed in schools."

"Oh, sure they are," I said. "Schools have janitors, don't they? And janitors sometimes live on the premises and often have pets. So you can simply pretend we're the janitor's cats."

She didn't seem convinced, but decided to go along with it for argument's sake. "It's just," she continued, "that people always look at me as if I'm some kind of weirdo when I come barging in there with my cats. It detracts from my reputation as a serious-minded reporter or police consultant. They probably figure I'm some kind of kook."

"But you are kind of kooky," I said.

She laughed. "I guess you're right, Max. Okay, now my lips are sealed. We don't want anyone to see us talking, or they'll send me straight to the loony bin."

And so it was agreed. Dooley and I would refrain from chatting with her while she did her business and we followed her lead and acted as her eyes and ears, since one person can't possibly notice everything, especially when they're engaged in conversation all the time.

We were admitted to the principal's office who greeted us

with a kind smile and shook his head when the fate of Allison Spence was mentioned.

"She was such a talented teacher," said the principal, who was an older man with a stoop and a frizzy head of gray hair. "And beloved by all, parents and students and colleagues alike. She had a way of inspiring confidence, you know. Even though she wasn't the most forceful person, she inspired her students to such a degree that they drank in every word. And that's a rare talent in this day and age, let me tell you."

"So as far as you can tell she had no enemies?"

The man regarded Odelia curiously, seated behind his desk. He had put on half-moon glasses and peered at her intently. "I thought Allison's death was an unfortunate accident?"

"We're not exactly sure what happened," said Odelia. "We're still investigating the circumstances of the accident."

The principal nodded, though he looked confused by this statement. "Um… well, like I said, Allison was well-liked, and as far as I can tell she made no enemies here." He paused and closed his eyes for a moment. "Okay, so let's back up for a moment. Are you saying that it's possible that foul play was involved in the accident that took Allison's life?"

"It's a possibility we're looking into," Odelia admitted. "Though at this point we don't have any evidence yet."

"Yet," said the principal slowly, and leaned back in his chair, placing his hands on his desk. "You don't have any evidence *yet*." He smiled. "I'm not stupid, Mrs. Kingsley. When the police come to my office asking me if one of my most beloved teachers had any enemies, it isn't hard for me to put two and two together."

"I don't want to imply anything," said Odelia. "I'm just trying to paint a picture of Allison's life so I can get a better idea of the circumstances of her death."

"Yes, the way a person lives often shines a light on the

way they died," the principal mused softly. "Okay, so there was one incident that shook me. That shook all of us, I should probably say. This happened a couple of months ago. A new student had been added to Allison's class in the middle of the school year, which is never an easy thing to handle. The student has to be integrated into a group of students who have often known each other for years. But I thought Allison handled it well. Until one day the pupil's parents came in and said they wanted to make a complaint against Allison. They claimed Allison had started an affair with their son, who was fourteen at the time. I told them this was very unlikely, since I've always known Allison as a devoted wife and mother to two boys herself. But they insisted. They found evidence on the kid's phone, and when they questioned him about it, he said Allison had made the first move, and they had exchanged lewd texts and even pictures. So of course I asked if I could see the evidence and they bluntly refused."

"So what did you do?"

The principal shrugged. "What could I do? I asked the boy into my office and I put the question to him straight. Told him his parents had come to see me and could he tell me what was going on. He claimed nothing was going on and his parents had simply got the wrong end of the stick. And when I asked Allison about it she got very upset and said the same thing the kid had told me: there was nothing to this story except a parent pair who obviously got mixed up about what their son had told them. Possibly he was having a relationship with another girl he didn't want them to know about, so he claimed that the texts were from his teacher, just to get his parents off his back."

"It's a troubling story," said Odelia.

"Tell me about it. So I got back to the parents and gave them an update and suddenly they turned around and said to drop the whole thing. Said they'd made a mistake and made some assumptions that lacked validity and apologized. It was all very baffling I must say. I monitored the situation as discreetly as I could, but when I didn't see any evidence of anything untoward happening in Allison's class—no other students came forward to back up the story of this illicit affair—I decided it was all a mistake and decided not to pursue the matter further."

"And this kid, this student, he's still at this school?"

"No, he's not, actually. A couple of weeks later the family moved away again and took him out of school. I think they said they were moving to Wisconsin. Which was unfortunate for the kid, since all this moving around and changing schools wasn't doing him any favors."

"And no other complaints were made against Allison?"

"No other complaints were ever made," said the principal. "And I have to say I'd totally forgotten about the whole business with that boy until you asked me the question just now." He frowned. "I do hope you'll treat this matter with the utmost discretion, Mrs. Kingsley. I don't want to tarnish Allison's reputation, which is stellar in every way."

"I'll be very discreet," Odelia promised, but I could see it had made her think that there might be something there. "What can you tell me about Allison's husband Barry?" she asked now.

"Not much. I don't think I ever even met the man. Allison dealt with her kids and the husband wasn't in the picture as far as I can tell. He was always very busy, apparently. A very brilliant and successful man, by all accounts, but not involved in the schooling aspect of his kids."

"Is that a common thing?" she wanted to know.

"It's pretty common, yes," said the principal. "A lot of the dads are too busy to be involved, unfortunately. But that's just the way it is."

The interview seemed to be over, and Odelia took her leave. But as she shook the principal's hand, the man said, "There's one more thing I've just remembered. I'm sure it's nothing, but I would be remiss if I didn't tell you."

"What is it?"

"Well, about a week before the accident Allison came in one morning looking very upset about something. When I asked her what it was she wouldn't say, but I had the impression that things weren't going well at home. I would have pressed her on the matter, but I could tell she wasn't prepared to take me into her confidence. But she might have told Mrs. Marlin. She's our English teacher. She and Allison have always been very close. More friends than colleagues, in fact. So if anyone knows what was going on with Allison, it would be Susan Marlin."

Odelia thanked the man profusely, and then we were off, to go in search of Mrs. Marlin, hoping to squeeze some more information out of her about the late Allison Spence.

CHAPTER 20

*W*e met Susan Marlin in the teacher's lounge, which was a cozy place where teachers could take a break, drink a cup of coffee and have a bite to eat or chat with their fellow members of the school faculty. After Odelia introduced herself, Susan took us to a corner near the window where we wouldn't be disturbed and we settled ourselves on a couple of couches that had been placed there. Nearby, the coffee machine was bubbling away, spreading the distinct aroma of fresh brew, and Odelia asked her first question. Mrs. Marlin was a fiftysomething woman with a thick tuft of gray hair piled on top of her head and a kind open face. She seemed genuinely sad about the loss of her good friend Allison, and said she was probably the best teacher she had ever known.

"Allison had a gift with these kids, you know," she said. "She got them somehow, and they felt that and responded to that. No one else I ever met had that particular gift but she did. And I like to think I'm a better teacher today because of what Allison taught me. Not so much what she actually said to me but just from being around her and studying her I have this feeling I became a better teacher myself."

"Lead by example," said Odelia, nodding.

"Yeah, she wasn't the kind of person who would show off or anything. She was very quiet. But when she spoke everyone listened, including the parents. And as we all know it's very hard for a teacher to deal with the parents sometimes, since they can be demanding and don't always get what's going on with their own kids."

"Principal Brown told me about an incident that happened a couple of weeks ago," said Odelia. "And I was hoping you could tell me some more about that."

Susan nodded. "Steve Watson, right? Allison told me about him. The thing is that Steve was mature beyond his years, maybe because he'd been moved around so much. Before they arrived in Hampton Cove his parents had lived in five different places so that means that Steve had gone to five different schools before he hit puberty."

"So what happened between Allison and Steve, Susan?"

"Nothing happened as far as I can tell, except that Steve started having these fantasies about his teacher. Now we've all been there. Boys that age sometimes get a little weird around their female teachers, and Steve being more mature had it worse than some of the other kids in his class. But this was something else. He started sending messages to her. Inappropriate messages I might add. Allison used to show me some of these messages and I told her to take them to the principal, since this was getting out of control. But she said if she told the principal he'd inform Steve's parents and he'd get into a whole lot of trouble, since apparently his dad was a guy with a real temper. So she just told Steve to stop, blocked him on her phone and that was it. But then somehow his parents found out about it and complained to the principal and that set off this chain of events that made it very difficult for Steve to stay in her class. At the end of the day I think his parents decided it was better to take him out of school and the last thing we heard was that they moved again."

"So Allison and Steve were never actually in a relationship?"

Susan's face spoke volumes. "Oh, no way! She would never do such a thing. I'm sure Steve thought something was going on between them, though. But then that's probably because Allison was way too nice to him and he probably got some ideas. We've all been there. But no, she never encouraged him or anything. Quite the opposite."

"Okay, so Principal Brown also told me that a week before the accident Allison came to school looking very upset. And he thought you might know more about that?"

Susan nodded. I saw she was wringing her hands now, clearly flashing back to the events that had transpired that day. "I saw it the minute she walked in. Her eyes were red and she had obviously been crying. So I asked her what was going on, and at first she wouldn't tell me. But finally she broke down and said that she and Barry had this huge fight, and she didn't think her marriage was going to survive."

"What was the fight about?" asked Odelia.

"I'm not sure. Probably about the fact that Barry was this crazy workaholic who cared about nothing but his work. He wasn't involved in the raising of his kids, or the household, or anything. Nothing but work, work, work, and frankly Allison was sick and tired of the whole thing. She said she might as well not have a husband if he was going to devote all of his time and energy to that stupid job of his. And look, I understand that his job is important to him, and he's a brilliant guy and obviously what he does is very important. But why get married and have kids if you're simply going to ignore them for the rest of their lives? Allison was right. She might as well have divorced the guy and raised those kids all by herself, which was pretty much what she was doing anyway." She pressed a tissue to her eyes. "I'm not sure if I should say this, but I have my suspicions about the guy, you know."

"About Barry?"

She nodded. "Don't tell him I said this, but two days before the accident Allison told me she had finally made a decision. She had been talking to a divorce lawyer and she was going to do it. She was going to divorce that man and she was going to take the kids. She felt it was her responsibility to make sure they didn't have to suffer living in such a toxic environment any longer. As a mother it was her duty to take them away from their father, no matter how hard it was going to be." She looked up. "She also told me that he would fight her every step of the way. And that he was going to try and take her kids away from her."

CHAPTER 21

Chloe didn't know what to expect from her 'coffee date' with Sidney Grant. She certainly hadn't expected him to be so courteous. He even got up when she arrived and pulled out her chair. No one had ever done that for her that she could remember. So either Sidney was a really nice guy or he was a little weird. The fact that he liked to participate in these eating contests probably pointed to the latter, but since she had vowed not to judge the guy before the check came, she tamped down on that particular habit of hers and decided to go with the flow for now.

"So you're an actual nurse?" he asked when she had told him what she did for a living.

"Yeah, I am," she said. "Why? What did you think I did?"

"Oh, I don't know. I just figured it was probably something creative."

She laughed. "Why? Do I look like a creative person to you?"

"You do, actually," he admitted with a sheepish smile. "I thought you were into the arts in a big way. Maybe like a writer or a painter."

"No, I'm afraid I have to disappoint you there," she said. "I don't have a creative bone in my body. During art class I always got the lowest grades in my class. I couldn't even draw a straight line with a ruler."

He laughed, and she had to say he had a nice laugh, with little dimples in his cheeks.

"So what do you do?" she asked.

"I work at Town Hall in the planning department," he said. "Though lately they've assigned me to a special top secret project."

"Ooh, that sounds intriguing. So I guess you can't tell me about it, huh?" She took a sip from her latte with extra cream and figured that if nothing came of this coffee date that wasn't actually a date, at least she got a delicious latte and a nice chat with an interesting guy out of it.

"It's not that big a big secret," he said with a shrug. "It's actually a little weird, I gotta say." And so he told her the story. About a mouse colony that needed to be shifted from some old factory to a new place.

"The old army base?" she said with a frown. "I think I know where that is. But are you sure the military will give you access to the place? As far as I know it's off-limits to anyone other than military personnel."

"Yeah, but it's been abandoned for so long I'm sure they won't mind. Anyway, Sharona thinks it's a good idea, and she usually knows what she's doing."

"Who's Sharona?"

"A friend and a colleague. We've known each other since we were kids. Our moms are best friends, so we used to play together all the time while they were gossiping about the neighbors. My mom and Sharona's mom actually want us to get married, but so far we've been able to avoid that particular fate. And in fact Sharona is getting married to a crooner soon, so it looks as if our moms' plans will finally be thwarted." He grinned as if it was a great life achievement to thwart his mom's plans.

"My mom doesn't want me to get married at all," Chloe confessed. "She figures all men are evil and should be eradicated as a species. She's been thinking about engineering a virus that would only affect the male genome, and then spreading it via an aerosol or something in the air."

"Your mom sounds like a real sweetheart," said Sidney.

"Oh, she's basically harmless. She is a biotechnology engineer at a chemical lab, though, so if she wanted to she probably could end all male life on the planet." When Sidney stared at her with dismay, she laughed. "I'm just kidding. My mom is a music teacher, and she doesn't know the first thing about creating a virus, so you're safe for now."

"Oh, phew. For a minute there I thought my final hour had struck."

"Though she does have a point that a lot of men out there aren't very nice," she said, and immediately wondered why she had said that. It wasn't exactly the kind of stuff you said on a first date! Even if it wasn't a date. Not unless you wanted to scare off your not-date, of course.

"Yeah, I see what you mean," said Sidney, much to her surprise. "A lot of guys out there are pretty obnoxious." He gave her a kindly look. "So... you don't have a boyfriend right now?"

"No boyfriend. Like I told you on the phone I had one, but he turned out to be a psychopath, so I had to end things before he ended me." Wow. That definitely wasn't the kind of stuff you said on a first date!

But Sidney, bless him, took it in stride. He blinked once, then said, "That sounds terrible, Chloe. Please tell me more."

And so she told him more, even though she probably shouldn't have. But he was so easy to talk to she ended up telling him the whole story. About how Josh had turned out to be this controlling creep, who wouldn't let her out of his sight for even a minute. Who read her messages and checked her phone. Who was jealous of everyone she met, even her sister Krystal. Who staked out the hospital just to make sure she didn't secretly meet guys. And who had even put a tracker on her car so he could follow her around when she went shopping. Finally she'd had enough and told him to take a hike. He hadn't taken kindly to that, but when she had dumped his belongings on the sidewalk and had changed the lock on her door, she figured he had probably gotten the message.

"He still texts me from time to time, you know," she said as she stirred the remnants of the cream into her coffee. "Says he wants to talk. That he's changed. That he's in therapy and he realizes what a jerk he's been and yadda yadda. But I don't think guys like that ever really change."

"Wow," said Sidney and gave her a sympathetic look. "Sounds like you went through a terrible ordeal."

"Yeah, at one point Krystal told me that if I didn't break up with Josh she would do it for me. She even threatened to call the police and have him escorted from the premises. But I finally realized I had to take action myself." She took a deep breath. "So I gathered all of my courage and did the deed. And I have to say I've never felt so relieved in my life."

"Yeah, I can imagine," said Sidney. He'd been using a straw for drinking his hot chocolate, which she had never seen anyone do before but which looked pretty cute. "I'm not saying Caroline was the same, but she was pretty bossy. She kept pushing me to enter these eating contests even after I told her I should probably stop. She figured since I was fat anyway, I might as well make some money out of it."

"Ouch," said Chloe as she winced. "That's not very nice."

"No, she wasn't. Nice, I mean. Well, I guess you saw what she's like."

"Yeah, I had a front-row seat," said Chloe. "Though I have to say you handled that pretty well."

"By throwing up all over you, you mean?"

She laughed. "No, I mean, you could have kept on eating, and finished first and made your girlfriend proud."

"I was never going to make her proud," said Sidney.

"No, I also had that impression," she said softly.

"Oh, well. What's done is done," said Sidney with a shrug. "And I guess we all learn from our mistakes."

"Sometimes we do and sometimes we don't," said Chloe, remembering that she'd had a couple of boyfriends before Josh who, while they weren't exactly in the Josh league, were still pretty bad, all things considered. "I'm actually considering not dating anymore," she now confessed.

"After the experience you had with Josh, you mean?"

"Yeah. It just doesn't seem to be worth it, you know. And I guess I'm afraid I'm just going to keep repeating the same mistakes over and over. I mean, when I met Josh he seemed like such a sweet guy, you know. Attentive and kind and funny. And then when we moved in together he just morphed into this monster, all of a sudden. It was so weird."

"And now you don't trust your judgment anymore, and you figure your mom might have a point and all men are basically flawed."

"Exactly! I mean, how do I know that the next guy I meet won't have taken Josh's correspondence course and will turn out to be even worse? It's very hard to tell."

"I know," said Sidney. "Sharona wants me to try online dating. But I'm not sure. How do I know the person won't be another Caroline?"

"You won't know unless you try," she said.

"Yeah, I guess so. Sharona said she's going to help me. I'm her best man, you see, so she wants to return the favor by helping me set up dates. But I'm not sure that's such a good idea."

"You know what?"

"What?"

"I think I just had a great idea."

"You did. I can tell from your expression that you had a great idea."

"Why don't we practice on each other?"

"Practice what on each other?"

"Okay, so hear me out. I don't know you, and you don't know me, right?"

"Right."

"So you could be a psycho. There's no way for me to know."

He gave her a dubious look. "Okay."

"And I could be another Caroline."

"Impossible," he said. "I've only known you for five minutes and I already know you're not Caroline number 2."

"But you don't know for sure. Just like I don't know for sure. So why don't we keep seeing each for a while, and try to figure out if you're a psycho, and I'm a psycho, and that way we can start building confidence for when we start dating for real? Hone our psycho radar, so to speak."

"I don't get it."

"We date but we don't date. It's like a human experiment."

"We date but we don't date. Right." He still sounded dubious.

"It's all about the practice, Sidney! You practice your dating skills on me, and I practice my dating skills on you, and that way we help each other get better at reading people. So when we're ready to start dating for real, we'll have the skills to separate the psychos from the good ones."

"Uh-huh," he said, nodding. "I see what you mean. So we date but we don't date. Like using training wheels."

"Exactly! And then once we feel ready, the training wheels come off and we're off and running again."

"Dating other people," he said, and somehow sounded a little disappointed when he said it. Which was understandable, of course, after what he'd been through.

She put her hand on his arm. "Look, I know this won't be easy, Sidney. After the experience we both had. But it's the only way to get better at this. It's all about the practice."

"It is all about the practice," he agreed. "It's the only way to get good at anything. Be it driving a car, playing the piano or dating. Practice, practice, practice."

"It's an opportunity."

"It is an opportunity," he said, nodding. He glanced up and they shared a smile.

"So let's do this," she said. "Let's practice dating."

"So how long would you say we should do this?"

"Until we feel reasonably relaxed about the prospect of dating other people. Right now I don't want to date anyone. Once that changes…"

"Same here. I don't want to date anyone but you." He blushed. "I mean… not for real, obviously."

"Obviously."

He gave her an odd look. "So… this practice-dating, what does it entail, exactly?"

"What do you mean?"

"I mean, does it involve…" He swallowed nervously. "Kissing, for example?"

She thought about that for a moment. "Well, it's hard to know a person without having been intimate with them. So I'd say that kissing is definitely on the table."

"It wouldn't be a date without kissing."

"Exactly."

"So…" He stared at her intently, then closed his eyes and started puckering up his lips.

She laughed. "Easy there, tiger. No kissing on the first date, all right?"

He opened his eyes again. "Of course not. I was just kidding!"

She wasn't too sure whether that was true or not, but at any rate, they were off to a good start. She liked Sidney, and what was even more important: she felt safe with him, which at that moment was something she desperately needed.

"This was fun," she said as she checked her phone. "I gotta run. So let's do this again soon, yeah?" She got up.

"So how about dinner?" he said.

"Sure. Dinner sounds fine."

"How about tonight?"

She smiled. "Now you're talking. I'll text you the address. Pick me up at eight?"

"I'll be there."

She clapped her hands together. "Our first practice date. Yay!" The start of a whole new adventure. No pressure. No strings attached. Just a fun evening with a friend.

She bent over to give him a hug, but somehow their lips ended up meeting for a brief but ever-so-sweet kiss. When she walked away she wondered how that had happened.

But it was fine. It was okay. It was all about the experience. The experiment. And so far her instincts told her Sidney was one of the good ones. She just hoped that this time her instincts were right for a change.

CHAPTER 22

*K*rystal arrived home from her shift and was happy to see that Barry had already made himself comfortable. He was lying on the couch and tried to get up when she entered, but she told him to stay where he was and not to get up on her account. She had hurried home from work earlier that day to let him in, but hadn't been able to stay. Now she was determined to get him set up so he'd feel her home was also his home.

She had picked up the girls from school and they stood at the entrance to the living room staring at the strange man on the couch, his head wrapped in bandages and the rest of him pretty much also.

"Is that a mummy, Mom?" asked Amy.

"No, it's not a mummy," said Krystal. "This is Barry. He's a friend of mommy's and he'll be staying with us for a little while. He's had an accident, which is why his leg is in a cast and so is his arm."

Barry waved with his good hand and gave them a smile. "Hi, girls."

"Don't be shy," Krystal urged. "Say hi to Barry. And then you better go to your rooms and start on your homework."

Amy and Lisa did as they were told and said hi to Barry then hurried away from him as if he had cooties. But they giggled as they ran, so Krystal thought they were probably going to be all right. She had already told them all about their new visitor in the car, but they figured she was joking until they actually saw the new arrival with their own eyes.

"I hope I won't be a nuisance," said Barry. "As soon as I'm feeling up to it I'm going to put the house on the market and find a new place to stay. Probably an apartment, since it's just me now." He winced as he said it, and she could tell that he was still in a lot of pain, and not just physical pain either.

"It's fine," she assured him. "You can stay as long as you like."

"So what did Odelia tell you, exactly?"

"Well, she said that your accident probably wasn't an accident at all. That someone deliberately forced your car off the road. And that if you hadn't been thrown out you would have died along with your family."

"I'm glad the police finally came around to my way of thinking," said Barry. "For a while there I had the impression nobody believed me when I told them about the other car."

"Well, there were no witnesses apart from you," she pointed out. "So it won't be easy to find out who that other person was."

Barry nodded and then settled his head back against the pillow. He looked exhausted, Krystal noticed, and figured she'd better let him rest for a while. "I'll start dinner. You just stay there and try to rest."

"Thanks, Krystal," he said. "I don't know how to thank you for your kindness and your hospitality."

"That's all right. Just make sure you get well again, that's all I'm asking."

"I'll do my best," he said with a smile that quickly turned into a grimace as he tried to settle himself so he wasn't in too much pain.

She disappeared into the kitchen to start dinner, and wondered if Barry would be safe with her. There was no way for these people to connect him to her, so she thought he probably was. Otherwise she would never have invited him to stay, since she had her own safety to think about, and especially that of the girls.

When her phone chimed she took it out of her pocket and saw that it was her sister. She picked up while she checked the fridge for inspiration. "Hey, you," she said. "So how was your date?"

"It wasn't a date," said Chloe emphatically.

"Okay, so how was your not-date?"

"It was great, actually. We've agreed not to date."

"Okay."

"I mean, we're going to practice dating on each other, which isn't the same thing as dating, exactly."

"And how does that work, this practice-dating?" she asked as she took a bag of carrots from the fridge and checked if they were still fine.

"Well, I'm going to practice my dating skills on him while he practices his dating skills on me. And then when we both figure we've become better daters, we can start dating for real. I mean, in the real world of dating."

She laughed. "And this guy agreed with that?"

"Of course. He's a great guy, Krystal. Or at least at first glance he is," she quickly added, hedging her bets. "He might still turn out to be a psychopath, of course, but that's the beauty of practice-dating: there's no commitment. So if he does turn into a raving lunatic who starts putting trackers on my car and tracking apps on my phone, I can simply walk away. No fuss, no muss."

"Okay, sis," she said. "If you're happy, I'm happy." In the past she'd had to help extricate Chloe from more than one toxic relationship, so she could understand why her sister was taking things slow with this guy. She was treading carefully, and she had a point. They had both thought her last guy was the one, before he had turned into a real piece of work.

"I'm meeting him tonight. So what should I wear?"

"Considering this isn't a real date I'd just wear something comfortable if I were you."

"You don't get it, do you? We're practice-dating. So we're going to act as if we're actually dating, so we should do everything we would do on an actual date, including playing dress-up."

"This is giving me a headache," she confessed.

"Am I making things too complicated?"

"A little. But as long as you're having fun, that's fine."

"So how is your houseguest?"

"Settling in," she said as she took out the cutting board and started rinsing the carrots. "The girls seem to be fine, so I guess we'll just have to wait and see what the police come up with. The moment they catch whoever was behind the accident I think we'll all breathe a little easier."

"God, this is just a nightmare, isn't it?"

"Nobody knows Barry is here, so we're okay."

"Let's hope it stays that way."

They rang off, after she had advised Chloe on what to wear for her date that wasn't a date, and Krystal smiled to herself. She hoped that at least this time her sister wouldn't get hurt in the process of trying to find love. If anyone deserved it, it was definitely her. She didn't know anyone who had a bigger heart than Chloe, so she hoped this Sidney guy, whoever he was, wouldn't break it.

* * *

DOOLEY and I traipsed after our human as she made her way back to the car. We hopped onto the backseat and for a moment we just sat there, the three of us, as we processed the information we had just received.

"So what does this all mean?" asked Dooley.

"I'm not sure," said Odelia as she put the key in the ignition but didn't turn it. She removed her hand from the key and sat back. "Okay, so Susan Marlin figures that Barry and Allison's marriage was pretty much on the rocks. And also, there wasn't anything going on between Allison and her student. It's possible, of course, that Susan was wrong, and that Allison was having an affair with Steve Watson."

"Susan admired Allison a lot," I said. "So she was probably prepared to believe anything Allison told her—even outright lies."

"But Susan seems to think that Barry killed his own family," said Dooley. "So maybe Barry is the one who's been lying to us all this time?"

"It's possible," Odelia allowed. "But unlikely. Uncle Alec sent me the coroner's report on Barry's family and the cause of death was drowning. He also told me that road conditions were terrible that night, and that particular part is a known danger spot. In fact Barry is the third person who ended up in the lake in that exact spot this year alone."

"They should put up crash barriers," I said, shaking my head.

"They will now," Odelia assured me. "And then there's this Silvester Muster guy visiting Barry in the hospital, trying to make him believe there was no second car, even though Barry is convinced there was."

"Barry's work is very sensitive," I said. "He practically works for the defense industry, so it's entirely possible someone hired Silvester Muster to get rid of Barry. He could have been the one who forced Barry's car off the road that night. Only he failed in his mission and so he dropped by the hospital to ascertain for himself that Barry was still alive."

"These are all valid points, Max," said Odelia, nodding. "And so I think it's important that we find Silvester and ask him some questions."

"You could always get your uncle to put out an APB for his arrest," I suggested. "And then when he's arrested Chase could question him."

"Chase is still busy with this whole drug smuggling business," said Odelia. "And so is my uncle. And I'm not sure if arresting Silvester is the best way to go right now. The only thing we have on him is that he impersonated a police officer, which is an offense, but not exactly the kind of thing that warrants an immediate arrest."

"He wasn't caught on that traffic camera you mentioned?"

"No, unfortunately he wasn't."

"Then I guess we'll have to pay him a little visit."

"But isn't that awfully dangerous?" asked Dooley.

"I'm sure he won't hurt us if we're careful," said Odelia, as she finally started up the car. "All we want to do is talk to the guy, after all."

And so she peeled away from the curb, and moments later we were on our way to Marginal Security, where hopefully they could tell us where to find the mystery security guard.

CHAPTER 23

"Sugar plum?"

"Yes, sweet pea?"

"Do you think we should help Max and Dooley?"

"You mean with this whole Lucifer business? I'm sure they can manage."

"Oh, all right."

Harriet couldn't help but wonder, though, if she and Brutus weren't shirking their duty by letting Max and Dooley take care of everything all by themselves. They were a team, after all, so maybe they should do more.

She and her boyfriend were reposing underneath the rose bush at the bottom of the garden. It was their favorite spot in the backyard, where they liked to spend most of their time.

"Okay, so maybe we can at least ask them for an update," she said, piping up again. "You know, show that we care?"

"I don't see why not," said Brutus, who had been lying on his back with his paws stretched out. "But you have to consider that it's mice we're talking about here, sugar buns. So what if they don't survive? That's the law of the jungle. Eat or be eaten, you know."

"Yeah, that sounds a little harsh to me," she confessed. This whole 'eat or be eaten' business was all well and good, until it happened to you, after all. And she had this vague notion that karma might not like it when they left their fellow creatures to fend for themselves.

"Okay, so when they get back we'll ask them," said Brutus. "How about that?"

"Yeah, that sounds like a good idea," said Harriet, perking up to a great extent. "We'll ask them and then we'll suggest that we pitch in. And knowing Max he'll say he's fine and he doesn't need our help, and that will be it." That way they didn't have to do anything, while still having shown karma they cared. In other words: the perfect solution.

And so she lay back next to her mate and was soon fast asleep.

* * *

NOT FAR FROM where the two cats were thusly reposing, a small creature stirred. It had been digging into the earth with its nose, looking for something juicy and nourishing to eat, but when the two cats piped up, it had pricked up its ears and had paid attention. When the fate of mice was being discussed, it was important to take notice, since the creature was a mouse herself. Her name was Olivia, and she was in fact Lucifer's better half. Not satisfied when her husband had told her he'd engaged the services of a cat, of all creatures, she had decided to go and see for herself. You can't very well leave the fate of your entire clan to a creature known for its cruelty toward mice. And as she listened to the conversation between these two cats, it was clear what they were up to.

Lucifer had clearly been taken for a fool. A sucker! These cats weren't going to save them. They wanted to destroy them! Eat or be eaten! But not on her watch!

So she tripped in the direction of the house, but not before making herself seen and heard by the two cats by screaming, "Help! I'm a poor innocent mouse so please help me!" As predicted, they couldn't resist the temptation and came after her almost immediately, eager to eat her with hide and hair. And as she ran to the house as fast as her little paws could carry her, she led them through the pet flap, made a U-turn in the kitchen and then hurried out again, using a small piece of wood as a wedge to lock that pet flap and make sure those mean horrible cats who were plotting to destroy her family couldn't carry out their dastardly plan!

Now all she had to do was find out who this Max and Dooley were and make sure they didn't go anywhere near her family either. It was a tough job, but Olivia was determined to see it through, no matter what! Her family's life depended on it!

Dooley wasn't used to riding in the car for such a long period of time. He didn't mind short trips back and forth to whoever Odelia wanted to interview for the paper next, but now he'd been in that car for half an hour, and he was seriously starting to feel nauseous. Cats aren't designed to ride in cars, after all. That's something dogs are more outfitted for. Dogs actually enjoy riding in cars, their heads sticking out of the window and their tongues flapping in the breeze. The thought of poking his head out of the window and sticking out his tongue didn't hold all that much appeal to Dooley, though. Quite the contrary.

And so after what felt like an interminable amount of time had passed, he asked in a small voice, "Are we there yet?"

"Almost," said Odelia, repeating a word she'd used at least three times in the last half hour.

"How much longer is 'almost,' Max?" he asked plaintively.

"I'm not sure," said Max, who didn't seem to suffer the same qualms he was enduring. "But not much longer, I'm sure."

He settled down on the backseat once more, and hoped he'd be able to keep his breakfast down for 'almost' another little while longer. It wouldn't do to throw up all over the car, since Odelia probably wouldn't like it. Humans rarely do. It involves having to clean the car, and apparently that's not such an easy feat to accomplish. Expensive, too, if you want to have it done right by a professional cleaning service.

Finally the car made a series of lurching turns and Dooley felt even worse. Suddenly he just couldn't take it anymore, and he said, "Can you please stop the car?"

"Are you all right, Dooley?" asked Max.

He shook his head miserably. "No, I'm not."

"Odelia, can you please stop the car?" asked Max.

Odelia glanced back, and when she saw that Dooley was clutching the backseat with all his might, she immediately pulled over and opened the passenger door.

Dooley made it out just in time to throw up against a nearby tree, and immediately felt better. Behind him, Odelia and Max had also exited the car, and Odelia knelt down next to the stricken cat. "How are you feeling, little buddy?"

"It's those turns," he confessed. "Every time you take one of those hairpin turns it's as if my stomach is turned inside out."

"I'm sorry, Dooley," she said. "I didn't think."

He looked up, and saw that they had arrived at some kind of compound. The tree he had thrown up against was backed by a chain-link fence, and as he looked over, there was an entrance gate with an actual guard.

"Looks like we arrived at our destination," said Max.

"Yeah, looks like," said Odelia. "I thought my GPS was leading us astray, but it was right on the money as usual."

They approached the guard, and after Odelia had produced her credentials—her police credentials, not her press ID—he told her to drive through and park in the visitors' parking in front of the main building.

Ten minutes later they were standing at a receptionist's counter, where a kind-faced woman was searching her computer for a man named Silvester Muster.

"He doesn't seem to work for us," she said.

"It's possible he quit," said Odelia. "The person I talked to said he used to work here twenty years ago."

"Twenty years is a long time, honey," said the woman with a smile. "But let me talk to a colleague and see what I can do. He's worked here for over thirty years, and he knows everybody." She asked them to wait in the waiting area, and for the next couple of minutes she conducted a conversation with this veteran colleague.

There were several magazines lying on a nearby table. Some depicted the latest guns as manufactured by the weapons industry and had a lot of good things to say about stopping power. Others detailed the hottest new surveillance techniques and ways to keep your house safe from burglars and other denizens of the underworld. Odelia picked up a copy of *Guns & Ammo* and idly leafed through it. It was probably a nice change from *Cosmo* and *Good Housekeeping*.

"So how are you feeling?" asked Max.

"Better," Dooley said. "I'm actually hungry."

"Of course. Your stomach is empty now."

"Do you think they have pets here, Max?" he asked. "Because if they do, we could maybe sneak some kibble?"

At that moment the front door to the reception area opened and a man dressed in military fatigues walked in, accompanied by two very large and very dangerous-looking dogs. In fact they were probably the biggest dogs Dooley had ever seen.

"Maybe you can ask them for some of their kibble," said Max. But Dooley could tell that his friend was probably kidding.

The man paused in front of them, and the dogs sat at attention, intently staring at him and Max, salivating all the while.

"I think they think that we're the snack!" said Dooley in a small voice.

"Better not look into their eyes," Max suggested.

And so Dooley stared at the floor instead.

"Silvester Muster?" asked the man dressed in the military outfit.

"Oh, hi, Mr. Muster," said Odelia, getting up to greet the guy.

He chuckled. "Oh, I'm not Silvester. In fact it's been a while since I heard that name." As Odelia shook his hand, he said, "I'm Jack Robbins. I used to work with Silvester, oh, some fifteen years ago now?"

"Oh," said Odelia, deflating a little. "So do you know where I could find him?"

"Sure. I think I've got his number on my phone. What do you need him for, if I may ask?"

"He's a possible witness in a case I'm working on," said Odelia, and made it clear she wasn't prepared to say more.

The guy had taken out his phone and soon found the number indicated. Odelia copied it into her phone and thanked the man.

"When Amelia told me the police were looking for Silvester I figured he was probably in some kind of trouble."

"Did he get in trouble before?" she asked.

The guy grinned. "How shall I put this? Silvester isn't

exactly the brightest bulb in the chandelier, so when there's an issue that needs to be dealt with he has a habit of opting for the nuclear option when the gentle touch would have done the trick. Once we had a client who wanted his wife caught cheating on him with some other guy and instead of simply following them around and snapping a couple of pictures Silvester went and broke down the door of the hotel room the woman was holed up in and ended up getting beaten up by her lover, who was a bodybuilder."

"Not exactly the subtle approach, in other words."

"No, subtle isn't in Silvester's dictionary."

"So why did he leave?"

"Who said he left? He was fired when it turned out he'd been accepting kickbacks from a client for doing a job off the books, which is a strict no-no for any employer."

"So what are you guys doing here?" asked one of the two dogs. Dooley had ventured to look up for a moment and noticed the dogs were still staring at them intently.

"Um, we're looking for a person," said Dooley.

"Then you've come to the right place," said the second dog. "Finding people is what we do. So who is this person?"

"Yeah, and do you have some of their underwear?"

"His name is Silvester Muster," said Max. "But unfortunately we don't have his underwear."

"You should have brought his underwear," said the dog.

"Yeah, without something to sniff we can't help you, I'm afraid," said his colleague. "Always bring something to sniff is the golden rule."

"My name is Max, by the way," said Max.

"Dooley," said Dooley.

"Rax," said the first dog as he took a sniff at Max for good measure. "You smell good, Max. What product do you use?"

"What do you mean?" asked Max, and Dooley could tell that his friend wasn't feeling entirely at ease.

"What brand of soap? Dove? Olay? Palmolive? It sure smells nice."

"My name is Jax," said the second dog, "and you'll have to forgive my colleague. He's got this obsession with soap, and keeps sniffing people and trying to determine what product they use." He turned to Rax. "Don't you know by now that cats don't use soap?"

"What do you mean?" asked Rax, as if it was the first time he'd heard of this strange phenomenon. "Of course they use soap. How else can they smell so good?"

"They smell good because they lick themselves," Jax pointed out. "Isn't that a fact, Max?"

"Yeah, Jax is right," said Max. "All we do is lick ourselves and it makes us smell good, I guess."

"Well, ain't that something?" said Rax, looking baffled. "You have to let me sample some of that saliva of yours, Max, cause it sure got a great smell. Hey, you know what? You should bottle that stuff and sell it. You could make a killing." He grinned when he said this, baring plenty of very sharp-looking teeth!

"Cats can't bottle their saliva, Rax," said Jax.

"And why not?" asked Rax with a touch of belligerence.

Dooley didn't think he would like to be there when these two got into a fight. They seemed to possess a certain aggression that was boiling underneath that civilized exterior but could erupt at any moment.

"Because no human in their right mind would want to rub themselves with cat spit, stupid," said Jax.

"Did you just call me stupid?"

"I did. And what are you going to do about it?"

For a moment the dogs squared off, and Dooley and Max both retreated as far away from the duo as physically possible in the confines of the small space that constituted the waiting room.

But before Jax and Rax could start laying into each other, their owner gave their leash a jerk and was off.

"Never call me stupid again," said Rax.

"I'll call you stupid whenever I want," said Jax.

Then they both turned and Rax said, "See you around, Max and Dooley. Keep smelling!"

"Yeah, keep smelling," said Jax.

"Thanks," said Max.

"Thank you, Rax and Jax," said Dooley in a small voice.

"Phew," said Max once the two dogs were gone. "For a moment there I really thought they were going to eat us!"

"Me too!" said Dooley. And then he realized something. "You know, Max? All of a sudden I'm not hungry anymore!"

"Good for you," said Max, but Dooley could see his heart wasn't in it.

They both looked up at Odelia, and saw that their human was smiling. "I've got him, you guys," she said.

At least something good had come from their ordeal.

CHAPTER 24

*I*t wasn't so hard to find the man we were looking for. He actually didn't live all that far from where we lived, in fact. His apartment block wasn't as accessible as Odelia would have liked it to be, though, since it was located in one of those gated communities you always hear so much about. But when she flashed her badge the guy guarding the gate that gave access to the community immediately allowed her in. He looked a little surprised when he saw Dooley and me, but that couldn't be helped.

Silvester Muster lived on the far end of the street in a very nice apartment.

"All his security work seems to have paid off," said Odelia as she admired the building. She then took a deep breath and stalked to the entrance and yanked open the door. Dooley and I followed her in, and hoped we would escape from this meeting unscathed. At any rate we were both ready to defend our human with tooth and claw if need be. Though after our meeting with Jax and Rax our taste for violence was at an all-time low and so was our confidence I must confess.

"Maybe we should call Chase," I therefore suggested when

Odelia checked the panel with the names of the residents. "He's very big and very strong, and when Silvester sees him he'll think twice about kicking down doors."

"Oh, you heard that, did you?" said Odelia with a smile. "Don't worry, we'll be fine." And she pressed her finger to the buzzer. Moments later a voice called out and she announced herself. There was a ten-second silence and then the door to our right buzzed, Odelia pressed it open and we were in.

The elevator took us straight to the top floor, and when we walked out, we saw that a man stood waiting for us. He was a heavyset fellow with a round head and a buzz cut. He was also wearing orange glasses for some reason, and had a white little beard that surrounded his mouth like a ring.

"Silvester Muster," he said as he shook Odelia's hand. He glanced briefly at me and Dooley but didn't seem to think much of our presence, and proceeded to invite us into his apartment. "So what is this about?" he asked as he led the way into the living room, which was sparsely furnished and reminded me of the kind of apartment a serial killer would feel at home in. I wasn't sure we'd make it out of there alive!

"I've been looking into a car accident that took place on Ford Road," said Odelia, taking out her notepad. "The victim was Barry Spence and his wife Allison and their two kids Eric and Oliver."

"Uh-huh?" said Silvester, who hadn't offered us a seat but stood in front of us, wide-legged and with his beefy arms crossed in front of an equally beefy chest. "So?"

"So Mr. Spence was the only survivor, and he claims that there was another vehicle present at the accident. This other vehicle was driving on the wrong side of the road and forced Mr. Spence off the road and into Sunny Lake, causing his wife and kids to drown."

"Okay. I still don't see what that's got to do with me."

"You visited Mr. Spence in the hospital after the crash

and told him that you were a cop," said Odelia.

Silvester didn't even blink. "No, I didn't."

"You were recognized by the security guard," said Odelia, "whose name is Harold Porter and who's an ex-colleague of yours from your time at Marginal Security. You were also caught on CCTV, Mr. Muster."

The guy didn't respond but just stood there impassively. Finally he frowned. "Okay, so what if I paid a visit to Mr. Spence in the hospital?"

"So you're admitting that you impersonated a police officer? You know that's a punishable offense, Mr. Muster?"

His jawed worked as he processed this. Finally he sat himself down on the coach. "Okay, look. I was there on behalf of a client, all right?"

"And what client would that be, sir?"

"I'm not at liberty to say."

"Oh, you're going to have to do better than that, Mr. Muster."

The guy was staring out of the window now, chewing on this. Finally he took out his phone and muttered, "I'll just be a moment," and disappeared into the kitchen, yanking the door closed behind him.

We could hear him talking in there, but couldn't understand what he was saying since he was clever enough to keep his voice down.

"What's going on, Max?" asked Dooley, giving me nervous glances. "Is he sharpening his knives? Is he mixing a beaker filled with cyanide? Is he filling a bath with acid to dissolve our bodies?!"

"I hope not," said Odelia, who didn't seem particularly at ease at this point either. "Maybe we should have brought Chase along. He's probably better equipped to deal with these kinds of situations."

"It's because he's a big guy," said Dooley. "And big guys

respect other big guys. It's the law of the jungle."

Odelia smiled and so did I. "If he does come out of that kitchen brandishing a knife I'm bringing out my pepper spray," said Odelia as she dug into her purse and wrapped her hand around said object.

For a few tense moments we awaited future events, but when the door finally did open I saw that Silvester Muster's hands were devoid of knives of any description and I think we all breathed a sigh of relief.

"Okay, so I talked to my client and he's given me permission to talk to you," said Silvester as he placed his phone on the coffee table. "But can we please keep this between ourselves? I mean, off the record?"

"I'm not here in my capacity as a reporter, Mr. Muster," Odelia reminded him. "So everything you tell me will have to go into my report."

He thought for a moment, then nodded. "I guess it's too late now anyway. The cat's out of the bag," he added as he directed a somber look at Dooley and me for some reason.

"What cat?" asked Dooley. "Max, what bag?!!!"

"It's fine, Dooley," I said. "There is no cat and there is no bag." I could tell he didn't believe me, but Silvester had started talking again so I tuned into the conversation. As it turns out he had a lot of very interesting things to say.

"I work for the same people Barry Spence works for," Silvester began. He grabbed a packet of cigarettes from the coffee table and offered one to Odelia, who politely declined. He then lit up one himself and took a long drag. "Motors & Rotors? I report straight to the CEO. Turns out that a foreign contractor is very interested in one of their projects. Don't ask me what it's about, cause I'm not exactly a tech-head. All I know is that they build helicopters for the military, and so when this contractor started sniffing around it raised all kinds of alarms as you can imagine. So they started looking a little deeper into the background of the people working on the project, and more specifically the project leader."

"Barry Spence."

Silvester nodded. "They thought he might be susceptible to being paid to sell the designs of whatever he was working on to this third party. Which is when they hired me to take a closer look at the guy."

"You're a private detective?"

"Something like that. After I left Marginal I set up my own shop. So I started digging into Barry's financial records, his phone records, that kind of stuff. And I also started following him around."

"So was it you who drove him off the road that night?"

"No, that wasn't me," said Silvester, shaking his head. "I don't know what they told you about me at Marginal but I'm not stupid enough to pull a crazy stunt like that."

"They told me you're some kind of maverick."

He grinned. "Okay, so maybe I used to be that guy, but that was a long time ago. Nowadays I'm a lot more careful. I have to be, since I'm my own boss, and my clients wouldn't like it if I took their money and didn't get results. Anyway, so I looked into this guy Barry Spence and pretty soon decided that there was something fishy about him. The kind of money he spent wasn't in line with his earnings. And he kept going on these long drives. I used to follow him around but that was all he did: drive around for hours in the middle of the night going nowhere and meeting no one. It was all very puzzling."

"I think his marriage was breaking down," said Odelia. "So maybe that's why he was going on these long drives. To think about his life and try to decide what to do."

"It's a possibility," said Silvester. "The other possibility is that he was negotiating with the buyer. And the reason I couldn't find anything on his phone records was probably because he was using an unregistered phone. But like I said, I followed him a couple of nights and he never actually met anyone, so whatever he was doing, he was careful."

"Did you ever find any evidence that he was in contact with this foreign contractor?"

Silvester shook his head. "Nope. But I think what happened on the road that night had something to do with this business. Either he refused to play ball and they tried to kill him. Or he sold the goods and they figured they might as well get rid of him so they didn't have to pay."

"And make sure he wouldn't talk," Odelia added.

"Exactly. He's disappeared on me, though, so I have no way of knowing what he's up to and who he's talking to."

"I know where he is and he's safe," said Odelia.

This seemed to surprise Silvester. "I think I just missed him this morning. I drove by his house and looked around but he wasn't there."

"Did you see the accident?"

"Unfortunately I didn't," said Silvester, making a face. "The one time I figured I wasn't going to spend all night following this guy around he went and almost got himself killed. My client wasn't happy about it, I can tell you that."

Odelia thought for a moment. "You said that he had a habit of driving around all night by himself. But this time he had his wife and kids with him in the car. Would you say that was unusual?"

"Yeah, I would," said Silvester, flicking ashes into his ashtray. "It's the first time he took them with him on one of his midnight drives. And when I asked him in the hospital where he was going he said he didn't remember and made a face as if his head was hurting so much he couldn't remember a thing."

"I think his head really hurt," said Odelia.

"Be that as it may, my impression was that he was lying.

Though why he would be driving around in the middle of the night with his wife and kids is beyond me. The kids had school the next day and the wife had to work. She was a teacher, and by all accounts a conscientious one, so she wouldn't have been up to take a tour of the countryside on a school night. Anyway, I was hoping the guy would give me some more if I told him I was a cop, but it had the opposite effect: he clammed up on me."

"I wonder why," said Odelia, as much to the security man as to herself.

"Beats me," said Silvester. "Anyway. Now you know everything."

"So what is your client going to do?"

"He wants me to get to the bottom of this thing, obviously. At the moment Spence is home on sick leave after what happened, but once he's back I'll have to come up with the goods or my contract will be terminated." He grinned. "Maybe Motors & Rotors can hire you instead. You seem to have gotten a lot further with Spence than I ever did."

Odelia smiled. "I'm not sure that's true. Seems to me you discovered a lot about him that I didn't know."

She said her goodbyes to Silvester, after he had promised to keep her updated on his progress and then we took our leave.

"We didn't die, Max!" Dooley said as we rode the elevator down. "He's not a serial killer after all!"

"No, the news of the man's maverick ways seems to be greatly exaggerated," I agreed.

"I wasn't kidding when I told him he did a good job," said Odelia. "It's a pity he wasn't tailing Barry on the night of the accident, though."

"Almost as if Barry knew he wasn't being followed, wouldn't you say?" I said, and exchanged a look of understanding with our human.

CHAPTER 25

*A*fter our day of interviews, we were finally home again. Odelia had dropped us off while she returned to the office to work out some of the stuff she had discovered and also to touch base with her husband to decide how they should proceed. I have to say I was happy to be home again. Traipsing all over town interviewing people is all well and good but at the end of the day I'm basically a homebody and I enjoy nothing more than to lie on my couch, enjoy a pleasant relaxing nap and dream of my next bowl of kibble.

So it was a great surprise to us when we tried to enter through the pet flap and found that someone had blocked the darn thing. And try as I might, I simply couldn't get it to budge!

"We're locked out, Max," Dooley said, sounding just about as surprised as I was feeling. "Now who would pull a dirty trick like that?"

"I have no idea," I said. The pet flap's operations manual is strictly in the hands of our humans, and so it stood to reason that one of them would have locked us out of home and hearth. To what purpose I simply couldn't fathom. Which is when I suddenly heard a loud cry coming from inside the house.

"Help," Harriet's voice was saying. "We're locked up in here, you guys!"

"Who did the locking?" I asked, very curious.

"A mouse!" Harriet's voice came back, which surprised me to an even greater extent. Now how could a simple mouse have the wherewithal to lock a pair of cats into a house? It just seemed like an extremely unrealistic assumption.

"Did you witness this mouse do the actual locking?" I asked therefore, interested in getting to the bottom of this mystery.

"Who cares?!" Harriet shouted. "Just get us out of here, will you?"

I studied the pet flap and discovered that someone had jammed a wedge underneath it, causing it to down tools, so I removed the wedge and the pet flap regained its former functionality. Immediately Harriet and Brutus zoomed through the egress and joined us on the patio.

"It was just the weirdest thing," said Brutus. "A mouse cried out for help, and it looked really distressed when it said it. So naturally we followed it into the house, at which point the creature made an abrupt about-face and ran straight out of the house again, locking the pet flap."

"But why?" I asked. "Why would a mouse want to lock you guys inside the house?"

"Beats me," said Harriet. "But I'm glad we're out again. You have no idea what it's like being locked up like that. We felt like prisoners, didn't we, snuggle bear?"

"Yeah, it was terrible," Brutus agreed.

I wasn't buying it. "But… you had everything in there," I argued. "Your litter boxes, your food bowls, plenty of water to drink, and the house is pretty big, you guys. You had couches to nap on, beds, carpets, the windowsill... I mean, it's not exactly Alcatraz in there."

Harriet gave me a dirty look. "You have no conception of what it's like to be robbed of your freedom, Max. No conception whatsoever. It's all about the feeling of being trapped, not some minor creature comforts nobody cares about."

"Yeah, the house is all fine and good," Brutus agreed, "but it's this idea that you're locked up and can't get out that beats me every time."

He had a point, of course. I also hate it when I'm locked up or locked out of some place, which is why Odelia mostly keeps all the doors in the house open, because when I see a closed door I just have to have it opened immediately. Call it nuts or simply a survival instinct to know what's lying behind that particular door, but that's the way it is.

"Okay, so that's what our day was like," said Harriet. "Now tell us about your day."

And so we told them about the investigation into the accident that had taken the life of Barry Spence's family. It didn't take us long to get our main point across, which is that it all boiled down to one of a couple of possibilities: either Barry Spence was a traitor who sold military secrets to a foreign contractor. Or he was so distraught about the pending divorce that he accidentally drove his car into the lake that night. Or he'd been the victim of the dangerous road conditions and a criminal lack of crash barriers. Or there was a fourth option we hadn't considered yet.

"I think he's probably selling secrets," said Brutus. "After all, the man is sitting on a goldmine of information, so he must have figured he could make a lot of money by selling that stuff."

"And I think he's probably guilty of the accident that took the lives of his wife and kids," said Harriet. "Allison was probably having an affair with this student of hers and when Barry found out he went nuts and drove her into that pond."

"That doesn't sound like rational behavior to me," said Brutus. "If he wanted to get back at his wife for having an affair, he could simply have divorced her. And besides, what teacher would be having an affair with a fourteen-year-old kid? That's insane, baby cheeks."

"It happens," Harriet insisted. "Some of these boys are very mature for their age."

"Allison's friend insisted that nothing inappropriate was going on between Allison and Steve Watson, though she could have been lying, of course."

"Of course she was lying," said Harriet. "Why else did Steve's parents take him out of school and moved out of state if nothing was going on?"

"I don't know," I admitted. "We'd have to talk to the parents of the kid to know for sure."

"Anyway, what I would like to know right now," said Brutus, "is what mouse in their right mind would pull such a prank on us." And he glanced around with a vicious look on his face, eager to find that mouse and subject it to a thorough interrogation.

And as luck would have it, just such an opportunity suddenly arose when a mouse popped up out of nowhere and appeared in front of us.

"Help!" the mouse cried piteously. "Help me, please!" And proceeded to run into the house through the pet flap.

Harriet and Brutus shared a look of surprise. "It's the mouse!" Brutus hissed. "It's the same mouse!"

"Okay, so let's follow it," I suggested, "and see what happens."

"Oh, I know what will happen," said Harriet. "We've been through this exact same thing before, remember? We'll follow it into the house and the moment we do, it will turn around and lock us up again!"

"Okay, so you guys run into the house, and Dooley and I will stay here and ask the mouse what the big idea is."

"Why do we have to run into the house?" Harriet said. "You go in and Brutus and I will stay out here."

"Look, it's all the same to me," I said. "But we better decide one way or another, since—"

"Hey, how long is this going to take?" suddenly a voice sounded from the pet flap. The mouse had reappeared and seemed put out by the lack of quick service we were providing. "I told you I'm in trouble, so you have to follow me and try to catch me. That's the name of the game."

"We won't try to catch you," I assured the little rodent.

"Yeah, we're not that kind of cats," Dooley chimed in.

The mouse frowned. "I don't get it. You're cats and I'm a mouse. So you run after me and try to catch me while I get away. That's the way it is, fellas. So don't mess with me, all right, and get in here right now."

And it popped back into the house. But when we didn't make to follow it, moments later it popped out again, looking deeply confused.

"Is this some kind of new strategy? Cause I'm telling you, it won't work. I'm way too smart for you guys."

"It's not a strategy," I assured the tiny thing. "It's just that we're not in the habit of catching mice. Like Dooley said, we're not those kind of cats."

The mouse scratched its head. "I don't get it. I clearly overheard those two over there talking about eating Lucifer and his family. So if this is some kind of mind game you're playing here…"

"No mind game," I said with a smile, since I now saw all. "You misunderstood. Lucifer came to us asking for our assistance in a matter of life or death. You see, his family is about to be evicted from their home, and he wanted us to find a new home for them, or try and save his old home."

The mouse continued to look deeply suspicious. "So... you're not out to hunt us all down and kill us?"

"Absolutely not," I assured the mouse.

"Huh. Well, how about that?"

"What's your name, mouse?" asked Dooley.

"Olivia," said the mouse. "And I have to say I've been around the block a couple of times, but you guys are the first cats I've ever met who don't have mouse on the menu." She still kept her distance, which was understandable, but at least she wasn't trying to trap us anymore. "So what solution have you come up with for Lucifer and his family?"

"There's a committee set up at Town Hall poring over that exact problem right now," I said. "It consists of three very capable people who I'm sure will come up with a solution."

"And I'm not so sure," Olivia shot back. "Cause we all know what those committees are about, right? Their sole purpose is to bury a problem and make sure it never gets solved. So if I were you I'd take this matter in paw and handle it personally. Cause before you know it the factory will be gone, and Lucifer's entire family will be dead, their lifeless bodies littering the factory floor."

"Oh, no!" said Dooley, turning to me. "We can't allow that to happen, Max. No way! We have to do something!"

"But the committee..." I began.

"Oh, to hell with the committee," said Olivia, who was a very lively and very passionate mouse indeed. "Either you handle this personally, or you don't handle it at all. So what's it gonna be?"

I sighed. "Okay, so maybe it's true that we should check in with the committee and see what they're up to. Get a progress report, you know."

"I've got a better idea," said the mouse. "Why don't you form a new committee to oversee the old committee? And then while you're at it, you can also form a third committee to review the first two committees. That way you can make sure that nothing happens. Wouldn't that be great?"

"Is that cynicism, Max?" asked Dooley.

"I think it's sarcasm," I said, eyeing the mouse closely. It seemed like a very intelligent creature, I had to admit.

"Did you use to work in politics, Olivia?" asked Brutus.

"No, I didn't, but like I said, I've been around the block a couple of times, so don't tell me how the world works, all right? So let's just get cracking and do this thing right now!"

And so even though I'd really been looking forward to having that lie-down on the couch, it now started to look to me as if that wouldn't happen any time soon. Instead Olivia had us head out to 'get cracking,' as she so aptly put it. What we would get cracking about, I did not know. But apparently she did, and so we followed in her wake.

"It's always the same thing," she grumbled as she led us out of our backyard and onto the sidewalk. "When you want to get something done, you have to do it yourself."

"Is that your philosophy of life, Olivia?" asked Dooley.

"Yeah, pretty much," said Olivia. "And also, even though Lucifer likes to live with his head in the clouds, I don't."

"Oh, so you know Lucifer, do you?" asked Dooley.

"Sure. He's my husband."

CHAPTER 26

I had no idea where we were going, but clearly Olivia did, for she headed straight into town, setting a brisk pace.

"Okay, so first exhibit," she said when we had arrived at an outside diner. "Sidney Grant and Chloe James. Sidney is part of that committee you're so proud of, Max." I could have told Olivia we were acquainted with both Sidney and Chloe, but my opinion wasn't required as she went on, "Now let's see how hard he's working to save our lives, shall we?"

Sidney and Chloe, seated at one of the tables, had picked up their respective menu cards and were studying the options closely, all the while directing surreptitious glances at each other over those same menu cards.

"Have you decided yet?" Sidney asked finally.

"Have you?" asked Chloe with a giggle. She put the menu card down. "This is fun, isn't it? I mean, it's so meta. To date but not to date."

"That is the question," said Sidney, arching an eyebrow.

Chloe laughed loudly at this, as if Sidney had said the funniest thing. "You're such a hoot, Sid. Can I call you Sid?"

"Oh, sure," said Sidney, simpering a little.

Chloe had placed her hand on his, and for a moment they looked deeply into each other's eyes, then Chloe pulled back her hand and said, "Okay, so I think I'll just let you decide. You're the man, after all, so I'm guessing that's the common thing to do on occasions like these, right?"

"I guess so," said Sidney. "To be honest I'm not an expert on the whole dating thing, you know. In fact I don't think I've ever gone out on a date like this before in my life."

"What do you mean? You have dated, right?"

"Oh, sure, but not like this. When I met Caroline at one of these eating contests, she came to see me backstage when it was all over and said watching me eat was the most exciting thing she'd ever seen, so she asked if she could be my girl-friend and I said yeah, sure, why not, and that was it."

"But you went out, right? To the movies and such?"

"Caroline didn't like to go out," said Sidney. "She was more into the whole Netflix and chill thing. Mostly we ordered takeout and watched her favorite shows."

"Uh-huh. She sounds like an interesting girl."

Sidney grimaced. "That's one way of saying it. Sharona said she was my personal dominatrix. She didn't even allow me to go to the movies with Sharona, so that was probably the reason she said it, but still."

"She reminds me of my ex," said Chloe.

"Yeah, the two of them should probably date."

Chloe grinned. "We should totally set that up. I'm sure they would be into each other in a big way."

They shared a warm smile, and hands were touching again, I saw. "So… what's supposed to happen now?" asked Sidney. "If this were a real date, I mean, and not just a prac-tice date."

"Well, like I said, you would order for me, and tell me what wine I should have with dinner, and what dessert I should eat, and you'd also pay for dinner and then take me home and decide whether we should go up for a nightcap or not…" She frowned. "At least that's what Josh would do." Her frown deepened. "My God, I'm totally following his script, aren't I? Doing what he would tell me I should do."

"Yeah, sounds to me like you are following his instructions for the perfect date," Sidney agreed. "So what do *you* want to do, Chloe? What would make you happy?"

She glanced around. "I could kill for a burger right now. I mean, I don't even like wine."

He laughed. "I don't particularly like wine either, to be honest. Or…" He read from the menu. "Steelhead trout roe, whatever that is."

She placed her hands on the table and her eyes were shining. "Want to get out of here and grab a burger at Louie's Diner?"

"Absolutely," said Sidney. "Thought you'd never ask!"

Just then, a liveried waiter arrived to take their order, and was surprised when they politely declined and walked away, arm in arm, to head down to the local diner for a simple burger and fries.

"See?" said Olivia. "They're supposed to save my family's life, and instead they're stuffing their faces with burgers!"

"I thought the whole thing was kinda cute," said Harriet. "Clearly we're in the presence of young love, and I don't know about you, but I happen to find young love invigorating."

"And I find it sickening!" Olivia cried, stomping her little paw on the pavement. "Let's go!"

And so we followed her to a different restaurant, this one even fancier than the previous one, where she introduced us to a different couple.

"This is Sharona Jordan," she said. "She's also a member of the committee that's supposed to come up with solutions for the problem that's facing my boyfriend. But what does she do? She eats!"

It was true. Sharona, whom we had met along with Sidney and also Julius Gibson, was indeed eating, there was no getting around that fact. But she didn't seem to enjoy her meal as much as she should have, considering her surroundings and the price the food must have cost. Her table partner was a middle-aged man with a paunch and dangerously receding hairline who was dressed to the nines but didn't exactly look like a man in the throes of passion and romance, as one would expect.

"And so I said, 'Vinnie,' I said," the man was saying while he cut into his steak, "'if you can't get me into Madison Square Garden, you're fired.' And you know what that two-bit agent told me? 'You're not at the point of your career where you should be in Madison Square Garden yet, Burt. You should stick to smaller venues and hone your craft.' Hone my craft! As if I haven't been honing my craft for years. Here I'm busting my gut and this guy basically tells me I'm not good enough. So I fired him."

"You fired your agent?" asked Sharona.

"Of course! If he can't get me where I want to go, he doesn't have the right to call himself an agent."

"But what are you going to do without an agent? Who's going to get you your gigs?"

"Oh, don't worry your pretty little head about that, Shar," said the guy, and stuck a big piece of meat into his mouth. The juice dribbled down his chin as he munched down with relish and I winced a little. I could tell that Sharona was also not enjoying the distasteful spectacle.

"So what are you going to do?"

"I'll get a new agent, of course. What else? And this time I'll make sure I get a shark. You need a shark to get ahead in this business, sugar plum. It's a dog-eat-dog world, after all. Aren't you gonna eat that?"

He was pointing to a piece of fish Sharona had discarded and relegated to the edge of her plate. "Um, no. It's still raw."

"Nonsense. Let me try." He leaned over and pronged the piece of fish and shoved it into his mouth then chewed it with his mouth open for a while, savoring the taste. "Delish," he said finally and with a big smile. The remnants of his meal were visible all over his teeth, offering a very unappealing spectacle. "You don't know what's good, Shar. This fish is just about the best I've ever eaten." He started picking at his teeth with his pinkie finger, removed a piece of fish and studied it for a moment before popping it back into his mouth. "Now what was I saying?"

"That you're on the lookout for a new agent."

"Oh, that's right. So I already got my feelers out, and here's what I want you to do. There's this agent—he's the absolute cream of the crop. Agent to all the stars. And I want *that* guy to represent me. If I succeed, I'm sure he can put me at the top. The thing is that he's a ladies' man, see? Married a gazillion times but still can't keep his hands off a pretty girl when he sees one. So I'm setting up a meeting with the guy and I want you to go with me, dressed in something real sexy. I'm talking low-cut top, cleavage, the works."

"You want me to dress up like a hooker so you can land a new agent?" asked Sharona as she took a sip of her wine.

He laughed. "Exactly! I knew you'd get it. And then at some point I'll go to the bathroom and I want you to go to town on the guy."

"What do you mean, 'Go to town on the guy,' Burt?"

"You know. He'll probably be all over you the moment I leave the room, so I want you to encourage him. Let him sample the goods. So by the time I get back, he'll be ready to sign me as his client."

Sharona's face had gone a little impassive, though I could tell she was simmering inside, and simmering something terrible. "So you want me to make out with this sleazebag so you can further your career, is that it?"

"Oh, don't be like that, baby," he said, trying to grab her hand across the table but failing since she yanked it back as if the mere touch of him was poisonous. "It's for the greater good! And if you won't do this little thing for me, what's the point of having a girlfriend in the first place?"

"You're such a jerk, Burt," said Sharona, getting up.

"Sit down," he said, his voice taking on a menacing tone. "You're making me look bad in front of all of these people."

"Yeah, well, you only got yourself to blame."

"Hey!" he cried, clearly shocked.

"Goodbye, Burt."

"Hey! I was gonna propose to you tonight!"

"Propose to this," she said, and picked up her glass of wine and threw the remnants into his face then walked off.

I watched her leave, and as she did, I saw that Julius Gibson, who had been sitting nearby with his mom, got up and followed Sharona.

"See?" said Olivia. "Another member of your famous committee, Max. Too busy with her personal affairs to spend time on the problem she's supposed to be solving. And that guy who just left and ran after her? That's Julius Gibson, and he's committee member number three."

"I know," I said. "We've met the three committee members."

"Who's the woman he was having dinner with?" asked Harriet.

"His mom," said Olivia.

"How do you know all this?"

"Because unlike Lucifer I don't trust these people!" said Olivia. "So the moment he told me that the famous Max had his case well in hand and everything would be all right now, I vowed to make sure he wasn't being naive as usual. So I've been following you around, and also keeping tabs on the committee. And I have to say I'm deeply disappointed, Max. Instead of saving Lucifer you've been so busy with this Barry Spence character that you probably forgot we even existed!

"I haven't forgotten about you," I said with a touch of defensiveness. "But the committee—"

"The committee is a bust," said Olivia. "All they got, as far as I can make out from spying on them, is that they want to relocate us to some old army base. Can you imagine my family at an army base? What are we, soldiers? Anyway, it just goes to show how useless these people are. So what are you going to do about it, Max?" she asked, having planted her tiny paws on her tiny waist. "How are you going to save my family?"

I had to admit I couldn't give her an immediate answer, and it made me feel a little foolish.

"We'll ask Odelia to call this committee to order," said Harriet. "Because clearly they've been spinning their wheels."

"You can say that again," said Olivia, impatiently tapping the pavement with her foot. "Time is running out, you guys! So you better get a move on before it's too late!"

And with these words, she took off after Sharona, clearly taking her monitoring mission very seriously indeed.

"She's right," said Dooley sadly. "We've been so busy with this Barry Spence business that we totally lost sight of our true mission: saving Lucifer's family."

"And Brutus and I have been very lazy," Harriet said shamefacedly. "Lazing about while we could have been doing something constructive for those poor mice."

"Olivia made a valid point," said Brutus. "But it's not as if we didn't do anything. We got Odelia involved, and she talked to Charlene and set up that committee."

We glanced up at Burt, who was applying a napkin to his face to remove the wine his girlfriend had poured all over him. "It's these humans," said Harriet. "They're all so caught up in their own drama they've got no time to fix the real problems. So maybe we shouldn't rely on this committee anymore. Maybe we should take matters into our own paws from now on, just like Olivia suggested."

"And do what?" I asked.

She shrugged. "What we should have done in the first place. Find a new place for Lucifer and his family and help them move."

It was an idea, of course. And as I pondered it, I suddenly flashed back to something Olivia had said about an army base. She might not like it, but as I thought a little more I figured it just might be the perfect solution. And the best part was that we didn't even need permission from anyone, since the place was abandoned. So I suggested it to the others, and they all agreed it might be worth a closer look.

CHAPTER 27

Since he got back from his boat trip Julius had wanted to take his mom to dinner so the two of them could have some time together and talk about the thing that was most on his mind. Address the elephant in the room, so to speak. His mom's disease was one of those things they never talked about as a family and he thought that was a pity. The thing was that Mom didn't want to talk about it, and neither did Julius's dad. Somehow they seemed to think that by not addressing the topic it would simply go away all by itself, which Julius knew was nonsense.

He gazed at his mom now, and wondered how it could possibly be that she was as sick as his dad had made out. She was so alive and so vital, so maybe the doctors had made some kind of mistake. He was determined to get to the truth, but didn't want to pressure her either.

So they went through the usual rituals of ordering dinner and enjoying some small talk, and they had both finished their respective main courses when Julius finally decided to broach the subject, since it was obvious it wasn't going to come up in the conversation.

"Okay, so what I wanted to ask you, Mom," he said as he glanced down at his empty plate, "is about what the doctor said. Dad told me a little bit about it, but I really wanted to hear it from you, you know."

"There really isn't all that much to say," said his mother, taking her napkin and refolding it. "Apparently I have a kidney that's not working as well as it should, and they've got me on this treatment that they hope will remedy the situation, and that's about it. Come back next week and we'll talk again is basically what the doctor said."

"But is it curable?" asked Julius, finding his mother's reluctance to talk about this frustrating to a degree, even though he understood, of course, and didn't want to force her to discuss something she didn't want to discuss.

"They need to run more tests," said Mom as she took Julius's napkin and started refolding that as well. "At which point they'll know more, I guess. You'd think that medical science would have all the answers, but turns out it doesn't. There's still a ton of stuff about the human body they don't know. Whether that's a good thing or a bad thing I'm not sure."

"So one of your kidneys isn't behaving itself, is that it?"

"Yeah, that's about the gist of it," she said with a smile as she finally placed her hands on the table and looked up at him. "Which is a good thing in my book because I've always been taught that we actually have two kidneys, and if one of them is being naughty you can have it removed and have the other one pick up the slack."

"So... your kidney has to be removed?"

She nodded absentmindedly. "Why are we talking about this?" she lamented. "You know I find it upsetting. Maybe we can discuss your Lucifer Coalition instead. Are you getting along with Sid and Sharona?"

"Let's stick with you for a moment, Mom," he suggested

gently. "If it's a new kidney you need, you know I'd be more than happy to give you one of mine, right? I mean, if it wasn't for you, I wouldn't even have kidneys in the first place since I wouldn't be alive."

"That's very sweet of you, Julius, but I'm sure I don't need a new kidney. Like I said, a person can live a perfectly normal life with only the one functioning kidney. So what is your plan? Where are you going to put those mice?"

"Oh, to hell with the mice," he said, a little more forcefully than he had intended. His mother seemed taken aback by his outburst, so he apologized. "I'm sorry, but in the grand scheme of things mice aren't all that important, are they? I'm sure they will manage whatever we decide. It's you I'm worried about."

"But there's no need!" she said. "Absolutely no need to worry about me. And that's exactly why I told John not to mention any of this to you or to your brother. I knew you'd start worrying and then I start worrying because you're worrying and it creates this whole big... *thing* and..." She frowned. "What was the question again?"

"Just let me come with you next time you go and see the doctor. I want to hear it from him. And I also want to be more involved in the whole medical procedure."

"But there is no medical procedure!"

He blinked. "You mean... You mean they can't... You're gonna... die?"

"Oh, no, you silly boy. I'm not going to die. Did you really think I was at the end of the line already?" She laughed a caroling laugh that was balm to his soul.

"But Dad said..."

"Your dad talks too much," she said, even though Dad was probably the least talkative person they knew. "Always shooting his mouth off about stuff he doesn't understand.

What the doctor said was that if I hadn't come to see him when I did, I probably wouldn't have made it. But now that I have, it's going to be all right. I'm putting it in very simple terms, and I'm sure Doctor Poole wouldn't agree with the way I'm telling it, but that's about the gist of it. There's still tests they need to run, and it's true my kidney is misbehaving, but it's all gonna be fine. Honestly!"

"Oh, so…" He swallowed away a lump. "It's just that when I got back from my boat trip, Dad said that—"

"Like I said, your dad talks too much. I'll bet he didn't even understand a word I said, and then of course he goes and gets all worked up about it and refuses to listen." She pressed a hand on his arm. "I'm not dead yet. I may not be as healthy as I used to be, but there's still life in the old bitty."

"You're not old, Mom," he said in a choked voice. "You're still young and very beautiful."

"Oh, now I know you're joking," she said, but her eyes were shimmering with unshed tears when she said it, and he knew she was just as emotional as he was. Finally she smiled and said, "You were always such a sweet boy, and that hasn't changed. So why don't you stop worrying about me and start taking care of yourself for a change, mh?"

"What do you mean?" he asked, dabbing his napkin to his eyes.

"You've never told me what happened between you and Allison, have you? So maybe it's time you told me the truth."

The last thing he wanted was to tell his mother the truth. Then again, in her position she heard all kinds of stuff from all kinds of people, so chances were she already knew.

So he sighed. "What have you heard?"

"That you punched Brian at the wedding. And Allison got so upset she took out a restraining order against you and got sole custody of the kids. So why did you punch

Brian? It's not like you to resort to violence, Julius. Your dad and I raised you better than that."

"I know," he said. And this time he was the one playing with the napkins. But instead of folding them he used them to create animal napkins the way he had been taught when he worked at the same restaurant where they were now sitting and enjoying a meal. This was when he was still studying to become a pharmacist. "And it's not as if I'd gone there to punch him either. I mean, was I mad at him for having an affair with my wife and lying about it to me? Of course I was. He was my best friend, for crying out loud. But for the sake of the boys I'd told myself to be on my best behavior. I didn't even want to go to the wedding, but Allison insisted that it was better for Eric and Oliver to present a united front. To show them that mommy and daddy were still friends. But when I showed up there—"

"Drunk, by all accounts," said his mom sternly.

"I wasn't drunk." But when she kept giving him that implacable look she had perfected so well, he relented. "Okay, so maybe I was a little drunk. It wasn't as if I was looking forward to watching my ex-wife exchange vows with Brian in front of all of our mutual friends. I felt like an idiot for even agreeing to be there, you know. As if by showing up I was giving their affair the seal of approval somehow."

"You were simply trying to be the bigger person," said his mom. "And showing them that what happened hadn't destroyed you."

"But it had," he said, pulling a pained face. "Of course it had. But anyway, when I arrived there I wasn't in a good place, and so I should have taken my own counsel and stayed home instead. But since Allison insisted, and I figured she probably had a point, I decided to put my own misgivings aside and put in an appearance." He squeezed his eyes closed for a moment as he remembered the day as if it was yesterday. "The first person I met when I arrived was David, Brian's brother, who was also a little drunk and very, very... spirited. Which is why he decided to tell me in confidence that his brother and Allison's affair actually started a lot earlier than they had told me. It didn't start that summer in the Maldives when Krystal and I caught them in bed together. Their affair started the year before, when we also took a vacation together to the Bahamas."

"Oh, I remember," said Mom. "Brian and Allison both caught a bug and had to stay in bed." Her eyes widened. "You're not saying..."

He nodded. "They did stay in bed. Together. While Krystal and I followed Raoul the tour guide all around the islands, our respective spouses had a great time. Which is what Brian's brother told me as if it was the funniest thing in the world. So when Brian and Allison exchanged vows, and talked about how happy they were to have found each other —true love at last and soulmates forever and all of that guff— I just got so mad, you know. At the treachery of it all. Cause David also told me about their secret meetings and even knew what hotel they used, to get together on a regular basis while they tried to decide when to tell me and Krystal—if they were ever going to tell us."

"And so you punched his lights out."

"And so I punched his lights out."

"Good for you," said Mom.

He looked up in surprise.

"You probably shouldn't have done it, but I can understand now why you did. If I ever caught your dad with his pants down with my best friend, I don't think I'd be as restrained in my response as you were that day."

"I wasn't restrained, Mom. I knocked a guy out cold in front of an entire congregation of people—our gathered families and friends. Not to mention my own two boys, who looked pretty stunned, I can tell you."

"Which is probably the reason Allison won't let you see them," said Mom thoughtfully. "Or even us—their own grandparents. She's probably afraid we'll tell them the truth about what their mom has been up to."

"Anyway, it's all water under the bridge. What's done is done, and at this point I'm resigned to the fact I'll probably never see the boys again."

"I wouldn't be too sure about that," said Mom.

He stared at her. "What are you talking about?"

"While you were on your boat, moaning and moping and talking to the fishes and the seagulls, I've been in touch with your ex-wife."

"You and Allison are talking again?"

"Through our lawyers," said Mom, and her face had taken on a grim expression. "I just didn't understand why she would cut us off from our grandkids—the only grandkids we have, by the way. And so I filed a petition against Allison's decision on the grounds that it constitutes mental cruelty to deny us access to the boys. It's been making its way through the court system, but our lawyer tells me he's heard some positive noises coming from the other side. Allison's lawyers must have told her she doesn't have a leg to stand on, and her lawyers have been in touch with our lawyers and an agreement will probably be arranged."

"What does that mean?" he asked.

"It means your dad and I will soon get a date and a place where we can see the boys. And if all goes well, it might become a regular thing."

"God," said Julius, bringing a hand to his face. He was overwhelmed with emotion for the second time that evening. The worst part of his indefensible behavior at the wedding was that Allison had denied Mom and Dad seeing Eric and

Oliver, something he felt even worse about than his own predicament. "Let's hope Allison keeps her promise."

"Oh, she will," said Mom, and he could see from the steely look in her eyes that she intended to win this battle. "If she doesn't, she knows we'll take her to court. Which is probably what you should do, honey, if you ever want to see your kids again."

"I don't stand a chance and you know it, Mom. Not after what I did."

"What you did? What about what she and Brian did? I think if you took your ex-wife to court and explained to the judge what led you to take a swing at Brian, you'd find him a lot more amenable this time."

"And why is that?"

"Because you're going to tell him what really happened."

It was true that the last time he and Allison faced each other in court, Julius had decided not to tell the whole story since he didn't want their kids to get the idea their mother had been having an affair behind their dad's back for a year. No kid deserves to know that about their parent.

"The damage Allison did to those kids by denying them a relationship with their dad is much worse than whatever they might hear about their mother's philandering ways," Mom argued. "So take my advice, Julius, and let me talk to our lawyer. And I can promise you that your dad and I will back you every step of the way. This isn't right, and we can both see how much you've suffered. So let's put an end to this now."

He gave her a grateful look. "I'll give it some thought."

"You do that. But there's only one answer I want to hear and that's yes. Is that understood?"

He nodded. And as he held his mother's hand for a moment, suddenly he saw Sharona stalk off past their table looking extremely upset for some reason. Then he glanced over and saw that a man was cursing and wiping wine from his face, looking very put off indeed.

"Will you excuse me for a moment?" he said. "I just saw—"

"Sharona," said his mom, nodding. "Go, son, go."

And so he went after his fellow committee member.

CHAPTER 28

*S*harona was so mad she could have hit something—
or someone. She'd known her boyfriend wasn't
perfect, but his behavior toward her now was simply inex-
cusable, not to mention probably punishable by law. In fact
she was so upset she stepped off the sidewalk without
looking and would have walked straight into the path of an
oncoming truck if a hand hadn't yanked her back to safety at
the very last moment.

The truck thundered on, the driver leaning on his horn
while he went on his dangerous way and when Sharona
looked back to see who had just saved her life she found
herself staring into the face of Julius.

"You have to be careful, Sharona," he said with a look of
concern.

"You're right," she said, and promptly burst into a flood of
tears. "I'm sorry," she said as he handed her a tissue and led
her to a nearby bench and gently sat her down. "I don't
usually cry without a reason."

"I'd say you have every reason to cry," he said. "I was at

the Cool Cucumber with my mom," he explained. "Was that man your fiancé?"

"My boyfriend," she corrected him, before correcting herself by adding, "My ex-boyfriend."

"I thought you said you were getting married?"

"He never actually proposed to me," she confessed as she dabbed at her eyes and nose with the tissue before rooting around in her purse for more. Lucky for her Julius seemed to have an endless supply at her disposal, for which she gave him a grateful look. "I thought he was going to propose tonight. I figured that's why he asked me out. Turns out he needed me to butter up some super-agent he's been eyeing since he fired his own agent. He actually wanted me to make out with this guy just so he would sign him and he could finally enter the big leagues."

Julius's face took on a dark look, and Sharona could see now how he would have punched his former best friend for stealing his wife away from him. "The man is scum," he said in a pithy response to her story.

"He is," she agreed. "And a very sloppy eater, too. I was thinking while I sat there that if I had to watch the guy eat like that for the rest of my life I'd rather shoot myself."

"Please don't shoot yourself," he said, and gave her a look of extreme concern. "When you stepped into the street right now, straight into the path of that truck, that wasn't... I mean you didn't..."

She stared at him incredulously. "I'm not going to kill myself over Burt Bradley, Julius! I'm not crazy!"

"Oh, phew," he said. "You got me worried there for a moment."

She smiled through her tears. "At least you got me laughing again."

"Guys like him aren't worth crying over," he assured her.

She nodded and sniffled some more. "I'm sorry I interrupted your dinner with your mom."

"It's fine. We said everything we needed to say."

Now it was her turn to give him a look of concern. "She's not… I mean she won't…"

"She's not dying, if that's what you're trying to say. Though I have to admit it's exactly what I thought myself, after my dad gave me some very cryptic comments to chew on. She told me the doctors gave her a clean bill of health but I didn't believe her, so—"

"So you figured you'd take her out to dinner and get the truth out of her one way or another?"

"Something like that," he admitted with a smile. "And as it turns out the truth was actually a lot less scary than I anticipated." And so he told her about the stuff his mom had revealed about the law case she had threatened Julius's ex-wife with, and how the upshot was that he might be able to see his kids again.

She placed a hand on his arm. "But Julius, that's great. You've wanted to see them for such a long time."

"It's not a done deal yet," he said. "But according to my parents' lawyer there's a good chance Jessica won't throw up too many hurdles this time, so they'll have their meeting with the boys, and then if I play my cards right so will I, so I can rebuild my relationship with them."

"Oh, Julius," she said, and felt overcome with emotion all over again. It was one of those nights, apparently. Or maybe it was the wine.

But before she could dissolve into a flood of tears, suddenly Julius leaned in and placed a gentle kiss on her lips. When she gazed into his eyes, he said softly, "I've been wanting to do that since I first laid eyes on you in that meeting room at Town Hall."

She smiled. "I'm sorry, but could you repeat that, please? I didn't get it the first time, I'm afraid."

And so there was more kissing, and she had to admit it was very nice. So nice in fact that when five minutes later a shadow fell over them and they broke the kiss and looked up, Sharona saw that Councilwoman Gibson stood regarding them with a curious expression on her face.

"Mom!" said Julius, moving away from Sharona as if stung. "I'm sorry for bailing on you like that."

"I can see you had more important things to do," said the woman who was essentially Sharona's boss.

"Did you… the bill… I was gonna…" Julius stuttered.

"It's fine," said Martha Gibson with a wave of her hand. "Consider it my treat." She smiled an enigmatic smile at Sharona. "Have a good evening, Sharona. See you later, Julius." And with these words she took off, leaving the two dissolving into giggles like two kids caught kissing, which essentially they were, except maybe for the kids part, though Sharona had suddenly flashed back to her younger years and so, she had the impression, had Julius.

And as they discussed Julius's mom's reaction, Sharona caught sight of a mouse popping up behind Julius's head. The mouse gave her a foul look, for some reason, then popped off again before Sharona could react.

It reminded her of something.

"I talked to the Mayor about the possibility of using that military base as a new place where we could house the mouse colony," she said. "And she said she'd discuss it with their representative. Though she didn't think they'd approve. They're very cagey about allowing any activity to be developed on any of their bases, whether abandoned or not."

"That's a short-sighted policy," said Julius, who was sitting very close to her and had wrapped his arm around her, which was very nice.

"I know, right? So I was thinking to simply go ahead and do it anyway."

"Do what anyway?"

"Relocate that mouse colony." She shrugged. "I don't see any other possibility, to be honest, and it's not as if the military will ever know that a couple of mice are traipsing all over their cherished bunkers."

"It's an idea," Julius admitted. "But we'd have to be discreet about it."

"Not to mention very secretive."

He grinned. "You're a dangerous woman, Sharona."

"And don't you know it."

"Okay, so maybe we can discuss it with Sidney tomorrow and make the necessary arrangements. Do you think we should tell the Mayor?"

It was a point Sharona had been unsure about. On the one hand the Mayor should probably be informed if they were going ahead with this crazy idea of hers. On the other hand she might not approve and even outright tell them not to go ahead, in which case they were stymied. Whereas if Charlene didn't know, she couldn't stop them either.

"Maybe I can ask my mom," Julius suggested. "She and the Mayor are close, so she'll probably know how she will react."

"Okay, do that," said Sharona. And so it was decided. Oddly enough, just then Sidney came walking past them, arm in arm with a woman who looked vaguely familiar. But then she remembered. This was the nurse he'd thrown up on. The one whose Facebook profile he'd googled. Sharona's jaw dropped a few inches before Sidney caught sight of her.

His face split into a big smile. "Chloe, this is Sharona," he said. "Sharona, this is Chloe." He gave her a sheepish grin. "We met at that eating contest I told you about?"

"I remember," said Sharona.

"So you're the famous Sharona," said Chloe. "Sidney has

told me so much about you I almost feel like I know you."

Sharona noticed how Sidney had been staring at Julius, and she could see the cogs in his brain working very hard. Finally she decided to help him out of his misery. "I broke up with the crooner because he wanted me to prostitute myself for the sake of his career," she said. "And Julius saved my life by pulling me from the pathway of this monster truck."

"It wasn't a monster truck," said Julius modestly.

"It was a pretty big truck. It would have squashed me like a bug."

"Uh-huh," said Sidney, blinking a few times as he tried to unpack all of that data in one fell swoop and failed miserably.

"Oh, and we came up with a plan to save the mice."

Chloe laughed at this. "Sidney told me about the mice. So what's the plan?"

And so Sharona revealed their secret plan to her best friend's new girlfriend and saw that she got Chloe's approval.

"I like it," she said. "Count me in."

"You mean..." said Sidney.

"I want to help you save these mice, Sid."

"Okay, great," said Sidney. "That's great."

Chloe turned to Sharona. "We're not actually dating, you know. We're practice-dating, and so far so good, right?"

"Uh-huh," said Sidney, who looked a little discombobu-lated, Sharona thought, but also happy.

"So let me get this straight," said Julius. "You're not really dating? So what is it exactly that you're doing?"

"Practice-dating," Chloe repeated blithely. "Dating is one big minefield as far as we are concerned, so we decided to practice it on each other. That way when we enter the actual dating field we'll be better equipped to handle things." She had hooked her arm through Sidney's and gave him a peck on the cheek. "For instance we decided to grab a burger today since we didn't like the restaurant we were at." She made a face. "Though I'm not sure what the dating rules would have to say about that. It's probably a big no-no, right?"

"There are no rules but the rules you make yourself," said Julius. "I mean, look at me. I don't know any of the rules since I've been out of the game for far too long, and even when I was in the game the only person I ever dated was my ex-wife."

"You married your first girlfriend?" asked Sharona.

"Yeah, I did. Didn't I tell you?"

"There's a lot I don't know about you, Julius."

"Looks like you guys have a lot of dating to do," said Chloe. "Or you could try practice-dating, just like me and Sid."

Suddenly Sid cleared his throat. "The thing is, Chloe, that I'm not sure this practice-dating is working out for me."

The woman's face fell. "What do you mean?"

"I like you, Chloe," said Sidney, whose face had turned very red indeed. "I like you so much that I would like to date you for real. I don't want you to practice on me and then go and date some other guy. I want to be that guy," he said, pointing to his chest. "I want to be your guy," he added, in case it wasn't clear the first time.

Chloe had clasped her hands together. "Oh, Sid, that's so sweet. I feel exactly the same way. I want to be your girl."

"You do?" said Sidney, much surprised.

"Of course, you silly doofus!"

And before Sharona's eyes, the two of them locked into an embrace and shared a passionate kiss. She glanced over to Julius, who was smiling, and he whispered, "If you don't mind, Sharona, I would like to try this practice-dating with you."

"Who cares about practice-dating?" she said, grabbing him by the lapels and planting a big one on his lips.

CHAPTER 29

J have to say that after the speech Olivia had given
us we felt so guilty we decided to spring into
action right then and there. It didn't hurt that the members
of the committee that was supposed to relocate the mice
seemed more interested in kissing each other than actually
doing their job.

"They're all kissing, Max!" said Dooley when we passed
the kissing couples. "They're all kissing all the time!"

"Well, maybe not all the time," I said. "And to be fair, what
they do in their spare time is their business. Working hours
are from nine to five, so they're off duty right now."

"Yeah, but still," said my friend.

"Isn't it just typical?" said Harriet. "Leave them alone for
five minutes and they're all over each other."

"They do seem very affectionate," I agreed as I watched
the two couples for a moment with interest. "Maybe they'll
get married soon?"

Much to our surprise, suddenly Olivia's little face
appeared from behind the bench one of the couples was
sitting on. She didn't look happy.

"See?!" she cried. "I told you! You can't trust these humans!"

In between some more invective about humans as a spent force, she did mention that the topic of the abandoned army base had cropped up in conversation again, presumably between two kissing sessions. And so I tried to boost the idea of the base as a new home for her family as much as I could, outlining its benefits and features like a veritable salescat.

Finally she had to admit that the idea had merit, and promised to run it by Lucifer and see what he had to say. For our part we told her we'd check out the base and determine its state of fitness as a new home.

And so as Olivia went on her way, we took off in the other direction. It was a long slog to the army base, which is located on the other side of town, but if we were going to assess its workability as the Lucifer family's new lodgings we needed to take a closer look for ourselves.

We arrived there in due course, and snuck through a hole in the electric fence, though I had the impression the fence wasn't as electric as it used to be. At least when my tail accidentally touched the iron wire no sparks flew and I wasn't charged with ten thousand volts of electricity.

The former base certainly looked big enough to house any number of mice I have to say. It was a sprawling complex that had once been manned by a nice troupe of army personnel. I didn't know what its function used to be, but we found plenty of barracks where people would have lived, and also a main compound with former offices and the like. I even saw entrances to underground bunkers with signs that made it clear no trespassing was allowed under any circumstances.

"This is probably where they keep their nuclear bombs," Brutus said admiringly as he sniffed at one such a door.

"Nuclear bombs!" Dooley cried in dismay. "But Brutus, that's dangerous!"

"Oh, don't worry, "said Brutus. "I'm sure they're not armed. You have to follow a certain procedure before those bombs explode, you know. Turn a couple of keys and push a couple of buttons or something. So I wouldn't worry too much about it if I were you."

"Don't you think it's dangerous for the mice?" asked Harriet with a shiver. "Mice like to nibble stuff, don't they? Wires and such. Imagine if they chew through the wires on a nuclear bomb and the thing goes off?"

"I'm sure there are no actual nuclear weapons on site," I assured my friends. "If there were this base wouldn't be abandoned. No generals in their right mind are going to evacuate a military base and decide to leave the bombs behind. That would be crazy."

But I still gulped a little as I saw all the Danger signs and the messages that trespassers would be punished. It didn't look very welcoming, to say the least. Then again, mice aren't welcome anywhere, but still they decide to stick around. In that sense they're the original rebels. So they wouldn't care about a couple of silly warning signs.

"There's a lot of greenery here," said Brutus appreciatively as we traipsed through a field of ferns. "Which means there's plenty of bugs, which will make the mice happy and their tummies filled."

He was right. The base, which must have been abandoned dozens of years ago, was totally overgrown with weeds and both plant life was particularly abundant.

"I like it," he said finally as our inspection round led us to what looked like an old army canteen. "I think the mice will have a field day in this place. Better than any old factory."

"It does look very accommodating," I agreed.

And we'd just come to the conclusion that this was an excellent idea when all of a sudden a noise reached our ears. Moments later headlights illuminated the derelict canteen and a van came to a stop in front of the building. Several men jumped out of the van and started moving stuff from the back of their vehicle to that very same canteen.

"Who are those people, Max?" asked Dooley.

"I thought this base was abandoned?" said Harriet.

"They look like soldiers," said Dooley.

And indeed the men were dressed in fatigues, and the stuff they were moving was all packed in big black crates that looked pretty heavy.

"Weapons," Brutus determined. "They probably decided to reactivate the base and they're moving in."

"I wouldn't be so sure," I said as I watched the men closely. I'd suddenly flashed back to what Odelia had said about drug smugglers present in our town and using it as a possible hub for their nefarious activities. Could it be that these were members of that gang and that the stuff in those crates was their unpleasant merchandise? It seemed more likely than the idea that the army would have moved back in.

"I think we better tell Chase," I told the others. "Because this doesn't pass the sniffing test."

"What sniffing test?" asked Dooley, sticking his nose in the air and sniffing deeply.

"It's just an expression, Dooley," I said. "I think these men are up to no good, and it's time Chase was informed."

"Oh, but if Chase comes barging in here with the police they'll lock down the base," said Harriet. "And then we won't be able to relocate Lucifer."

She was right. If these were indeed drug people, and the police arrested them, there would be a big hullaballoo about the whole thing. The army might decide that security on their base was too lax.

"At any rate, it doesn't matter," said Brutus. "Nobody is going to notice a couple of mice. Lucifer is very discreet."

"They won't notice a couple of mice," I said. "But twenty million isn't a couple, Brutus. That's a lot of mice."

For a moment we were stymied, wondering how to proceed. We couldn't let these drug dealers go about their lethal business, but on the other hand they might be the perfect neighbors for a family of mice since they wouldn't go around trying to hunt the mice since by nature drug dealers are very shy and don't like to draw attention to themselves.

But before we could decide, the decision was taken out of our paws by the arrival of Olivia and Lucifer in person!

"Oh, hi, Max," said Lucifer, giving me a happy look. He was glancing around. "This is the perfect place!"

"Didn't I tell you?" said Olivia. She gave me a pat on the leg. "Thanks, Max. I knew you'd come through for us."

"The only problem is those men over there," said Brutus. "I think they're army, but Max seems to think they're drug dealers."

"Oh, who cares?" said Olivia. "We're used to cohabiting with humans. We'll just have to make some adjustments. If we keep out of their way and they keep out of our way, we'll be able to live together just fine."

It was a philosophy that had served mice as a species very well over the past couple of million years, and had caused them to thrive.

"Okay, move in, people!" suddenly Lucifer yelled. And before our very eyes, mice suddenly burst onto the scene by the thousands!

"Oh, my God," said Dooley. "You brought your whole family along, Lucifer?"

"Of course," said Lucifer. "When Olivia told me that you guys came through for us and found this great new place to live, I figured there's no time like the present. So I gathered the entire clan in the factory's main hall and told them the time had finally come for us as a family to move out. And so here we are." He proudly gestured to the sea of mice. "Max, Dooley, Brutus, Harriet—meet the family. Family, meet my friends."

And so for perhaps the first time in history, four cats were actually instrumental in relodging a family of mice—with a little help from the Lucifer Coalition. It wasn't the kind of thing I was going to boast about to my fellow cats, but I still felt a powerful sense of pride as the mice spread out across their new domain and started inspecting it.

"They like it," said Lucifer proudly. "It's even better than the old place."

"It does have everything," I said. "And Brutus tells me it's got plenty of food."

"Oh, yeah, this is just great," he said.

We glanced over to the men unloading the van, and as a group of mice approached the canteen I wondered how the drug smugglers—if that's what they were—would react to the presence of their new neighbors.

Suddenly loud screams of terror could be heard as the men spotted the sea of mice streaming in their direction. Before long they had all retreated back to the safety of their van as the mice set paw for the canteen, possibly in a bid to secure the best bunk beds for themselves.

"Look at the kids," said Lucifer affectionately. "You can tell they're over the moon." He turned to me. "I can't thank you enough, Max. You're a lifesaver. You really are, buddy."

"That's all right, Lucifer," I said. "Anything I can do for my fellow man. Or mouse. Or whatever. And let's not forget that the initial idea actually came from the people on the Lucifer Coalition."

"The kissing couples," Olivia clarified for her husband's sake.

"Oh, right," said Lucifer with a grin. "Well, humans have their uses."

The men inside the van had now taken out their guns, it would appear, and had started shooting at the mice. Luckily mice are very agile and very quick to adapt, and before long they had all disappeared, before surging back again. It was interesting to watch. They moved like waves.

"Those guys are shooting at you!" said Brutus.

"Oh, it's fine," said Lucifer. "My kids can take care of themselves. They probably think it's a game and are laughing their little asses off."

There was more shooting, and all of a sudden one of the men in the van threw something at the mice, who threw it right back at them.

"See? A fun game for the whole family," said Lucifer proudly.

A loud bang sounded as the grenade exploded inside the van, and smoke now poured from the vehicle as men started to crawl out, coughing and not looking their best.

"Ah, this is the life," said Lucifer, filling his lungs and expelling a breath of happiness.

Moments later the sound of police sirens filled the air.

"One of the neighbors must have heard the explosion," Brutus suggested as we watched impassively as the drug smugglers lay on the ground, groaning and retching and generally having been dinged up a little by their own grenade.

"Drugs aren't healthy, Max," said Dooley, reiterating a public service announcement that these guys had probably neglected to adhere to. "They'll get you every time."

They had certainly gotten these guys. Police cars now swarmed the scene, and I recognized Uncle Alec and also Chase. Both men were dressed in funny-looking outfits.

"Bulletproof vests," Brutus knew. "To protect them from being shot."

There was no danger of that, since the gang of drug people had all passed out next to their burned-out van.

"Ambulance!" Uncle Alec shouted. "We need an ambulance!"

Chase had opened one of the crates and whistled through his teeth. "Looks like we got them, all right," he said.

Uncle Alec joined him and both men studied the contents of that case. They picked out a bag filled with something white and Dooley speculated, "Sugar, you think, Max?"

"I kinda doubt it, Dooley," I said.

Chase picked another bag from the crate, this one filled with little pills.

"Where are your kids, Lucifer?" suddenly Harriet asked. She glanced around. "Lucifer? Olivia?"

But try as we might, of Lucifer and Olivia there was no trace, and neither of their prolific offspring.

"They're very clever, aren't they, Max?" said Dooley with a smile. "At the first sign of danger, they go into hiding."

"They are very clever," I agreed. And somehow I had the impression that Lucifer and Olivia and their family would settle in at the old army base just fine. Especially now that Chase and Uncle Alec would make sure that the real vermin was safely removed from the scene.

CHAPTER 30

rystal watched as Barry tried to eat. Judging from his grimaces it wasn't easy, but when she tried to help him, he refused and said he had to learn to do it alone sometime.

The girls had gone to bed and now it was just the two of them at the kitchen table.

"I'm sorry you have to put up with this, Krystal," said Barry finally. "And I'm sorry for all the trouble I'm causing you and the girls."

She nodded. "The thing, Barry, is that we need to talk."

"Oh?" He had finally managed to finish the plate of pasta she had put in front of him and wiped his lips with a napkin.

"I talked to Odelia on the phone just now, and she told me about this guy she talked to today. He works for your company as some kind of private detective. They hired him since they believe you might be selling corporate secrets to a foreign contractor."

He glanced up at her and seemed genuinely dumbfounded by the accusation. "Motors & Rotors hired someone to spy on me? But that's outrageous. I would never sell my company's secrets."

"I know, but that's what they seem to think." She had picked up her phone and was playing with it for a moment before putting it down again. "So they had this guy go through your bank account and your phone records and everything, hoping to find some evidence that you are a traitor, basically."

"My God," he said, shaking his head. He looked pained, and this time it wasn't from the actual physical pain of his injuries but from the suspicions his own employers seemed to harbor against him. "The lack of trust is just staggering," he said. "They could have simply asked me."

"When people decide to sell trade secrets to a foreign power they're usually not forthcoming about it," said Krystal.

Barry smiled. "At least you've got a sense of humor about it." He fixed her with an imploring look. "I'm not a traitor, Krystal, you have to believe me. I didn't sell anything to anyone. No one even approached me, and if they had I would have turned them down. I'm not that guy."

"I know," she said calmly. "I know you're not that guy, Barry, and the man they hired to prove it didn't find any evidence, so you're off the hook."

"Well, phew," he said.

"Which leaves the question what happened the night you drove your car into the lake."

"I told you what happened. Another car forced me off the road. Someone out there is trying to get me, Krystal. I'm being targeted, and possibly it's the same people trying to buy these secrets. Maybe they figure if they can scare me enough I'll sell. Or maybe it's actually this guy who's been hired to follow me around. Maybe he made a mistake and caused the accident."

Krystal smiled and gazed into Barry's face. She liked him,

even though it was clear to her now that he was carrying a big secret. A secret so big he was prepared to go to great lengths to bury it, even going so far as to invent an entire story about being hunted by this mystery driver.

"Look, Barry, I think it's time you told me the truth," she said therefore. "I know Allison was going to leave you and take the kids."

"What are you talking about?" he said, but her words seemed to have had a profound effect on him. He had sort of crumpled in on himself.

"I know you spread a rumor that she was having an affair with a student of hers, hoping it would prevent her from getting custody of the kids in case she went ahead with the divorce," said Krystal. "But even Allison's colleague said there was simply no merit to the story, and I don't think a judge would have believed it either." She had placed a hand on his arm and massaged it gently. "How did you do it? How did you plant those messages on the kid's phone?"

Barry had softly started weeping, his whole body shaking. "It wasn't hard," he said, wiping at his tears. "All I had to do was figure out Allison's passcode to unlock her phone and send those messages to make it look as if she was having an affair with the kid."

"That was a pretty terrible thing to do, Barry."

"I know," he said. "And I hate myself for doing it. But I was desperate. She threatened to take the boys to Europe. She's Spanish by birth, and she still has family over there. So she was going to move there after the divorce with the boys, which meant I probably would never see them again. And I just couldn't have that, could I?"

"And she found out about what you did, didn't she?"

He nodded tearfully. "She said it was low. The kid ended up having to move away with his parents, and her reputation took a pretty serious dent, even though a lot of her colleagues refused to believe the rumors. But it just made her even more determined to go through with the divorce. And so…" He lifted his head for a moment, and Krystal could see how haunted the man was, how devastated. "And so that night I…"

"You drugged them," she said. "You put something in their food that knocked them out and then you put them in the car and drove the car into the lake, wanting to end it all."

"I did, but something went wrong," he said. "I should have died that night, along with my family, but somehow I was thrown from the car and knocked my head against a rock." He was wailing now, a piteous sight. "When I woke up in the hospital I thought I was hallucinating. I should have died, but instead I was the only one who survived. It was terrible."

"So you killed your family and you tried to kill yourself but you failed."

He was shaking. "It wasn't supposed to be this way. I loved them so, so much. I just couldn't let them leave. She shouldn't have threatened to take my boys away from me."

"It's all right, Barry," she said. "It's good that you're finally able to admit what happened."

"I did leave, you know," he said, becoming calmer. "I mixed something in their meal and then I left, even though Allison begged me not to go. She must have sensed that something terrible was going to happen. When I walked back in they were knocked out, all three of them. So I dragged them into the car and I ended up driving around for hours, not knowing what to do. I just couldn't bring myself to do what I had planned to do. I don't know what finally decided me. I just felt so tired. This had been going on for months. The fights and the arguments and the endless recriminations. I just couldn't take it anymore."

Odelia had quietly entered the room, along with a police officer. But when Barry looked up and saw them, he wasn't surprised. He glanced down at the phone lying in front of him on the table and then up at Krystal. "They heard?" he asked in a croaky voice.

Krystal nodded. "Yes, we heard everything, Barry," said Odelia. "And I think you better come with us now, if that's okay with you."

He winced. "I'm sorry, Krystal. I like you, you know. But..."

"I know," she said softly, and helped him out of his chair and to the door. She had arranged with Odelia that she would accompany them to the hospital, where he would be admitted in a secure wing. They would have to monitor him closely so he didn't commit an act of desperation. She felt he probably shouldn't be in prison, but then he had killed his wife and kids, so there wasn't a lot she could do about the fate that awaited him.

"What's going to happen to him?" she asked Odelia as they watched him being escorted into the hospital by two orderlies.

"He'll probably get a psych evaluation," said Odelia. "To determine whether he's fit to stand trial."

"He's been in a great deal of pain for a very long time," said Krystal, whose heart bled. It hadn't been hard to decide when Odelia asked for her cooperation. With two kids of her own she was appalled by what Barry had done. But she also understood he was a sick man, and suffering.

"I know," said Odelia. "And I'm sure his mental state will be taken into consideration. But he can't escape the consequences of what he did, Krystal. And what he did is terrible. He took the lives of an innocent woman and two children. And all because she threatened to leave him."

She nodded. Then remembered she had left her girls with her sister at home, and suddenly couldn't wait to get back to them. She and Odelia hugged, and the two women promised each other to keep in touch. It was probably the toughest thing Krystal had ever had to do, but as Odelia had explained it to her, she was probably the only person who could have gotten Barry to confess. To cut through the lies he had told himself and get to the awful truth.

She arrived home to find Chloe on the couch with Sidney, watching television together and very much looking like a couple in love.

"They're sleeping like a rose," said Chloe.

Krystal hurried to check on her babies, and when she found them asleep as her sister had indicated, she breathed a sigh of relief. She bent over their beds one by one and feathered a kiss on the tops of their heads before sneaking out of the room again.

She found Sidney standing around a little uncomfortably. "I'm so sorry for the intrusion, Mrs. James," he said. "But I happened to be with Chloe when she got your call, so…"

"And so I figured you might as well meet the man I've been talking about," Chloe said with a grin. But when she saw her sister's serious expression she must have realized now probably wasn't the time. "Are you all right?"

"I had a rough night," Krystal confessed. But since she didn't want to spoil her sister's night, she gave her a weak smile. "I'll tell you all about it tomorrow, if that's all right." And as she escorted them to the door, she whispered, "And then you can tell me all about your date with Sidney."

After she said goodbye to her sister and Sidney, she collapsed on the couch and had a good cry. It just showed her right for having a big heart, she thought, and falling for the wrong guys time after time. But as she stood brushing her teeth ten minutes later before turning in for the night, she knew she would get over this. And at least she had found out what kind of man he was now and not five years from now, when he might have tried to do the same thing to her and her daughters that he had done to his family.

The door to the bathroom opened and Amy walked in, rubbing her eyes and clutching a teddy bear in one hand. "Mom, I can't sleep," she said. Lisa wasn't too far behind, also lamenting that she couldn't sleep.

Which is how Krystal found herself bookended by two blond angels five minutes later, the three of them peacefully asleep in the big bed and dreaming of better days.

CHAPTER 31

Sharona wondered why she was being called into the Mayor's office. When she arrived there she saw she wasn't the only one but that Sidney was also waiting on the bench located in the corridor. The Mayor's door was still firmly closed, and so she took a seat next to her best friend.

"What's going on?" she asked. "I thought we had a committee meeting this morning, but instead I got an email to present myself here."

"Me too," said Sidney, who looked about as nervous as she was feeling. Being called upon to meet with the Mayor was never a fun prospect, since it often heralded bad news. The last time she remembered one of their colleagues getting such an invitation they had received a reprimand that had stung something terrific.

"So how was your date last night?" asked Sidney.

Sharona grinned. "As you probably saw for yourself it was pretty great. I hadn't expected it, you know. First breaking up with Burt, and then Julius was simply so... so..." She waved her hands in the air to try and describe how wonderful Julius was, but words failed her.

"I know," said Sidney with a grin. "My own date went pretty great, too. I didn't know practice-dating could be this much fun." But then his face sagged. "Have you heard about what happened to Chloe's sister, though? Her patient turned out to be a murderer."

"What?" said Sharona, sitting bolt upright at this piece of news. "You mean that nice man that was staying with her? The architect?"

"I think he's a helicopter engineer, actually. But yeah, that guy. Turns out he killed his wife and kids. Drowned them in the lake. And he was supposed to drown himself, too, only he ended up in the hospital, unconscious. You can imagine how he felt when he woke up and discovered that he was still alive and his family was dead."

"My God," said Sharona, clutching at her face. "So how is Chloe's sister holding up? She's got two kids of her own, doesn't she?"

"She does. Chloe and I babysat for them last night. They're great. But yeah, she's pretty shocked, I can tell you."

"So how did they find out?"

But at that moment a third person joined them in the form of Julius, and Sharona gave him a starry-eyed smile.

"Hey, you," she said.

"Hey, yourself," said Julius, giving her a warm smile in return. He lowered himself onto the bench next to the others and said, "So what's this all about?"

"No idea," said Sidney. "But it can't be good."

"It's probably got something to do with the project," Sharona ventured. "They must have some additional information for us, maybe, or something changed or whatever."

"Or we didn't do a good job and now she's going to fire us," said Sidney, who had a tendency to go for the gloomy prospect.

"Maybe she wants to give us a medal?" Sharona suggested.

Contrary to Sidney she liked to take a positive view of things. "You know, for services rendered?"

"What service did we render, though?" said Sidney. "We haven't even started on the project yet."

"Oh, yes, we have," said Julius. "We found a location for the rats."

"Mice," Sharona corrected him.

"Right. So now all we have to do is get in touch with the MOD and try and get them to play ball."

"Good luck with that," said Sidney.

At that moment the door to the inner sanctum opened and the Mayor herself appeared. She gave them a stern-faced look and Sharona's insides momentarily turned to jelly before miraculously solidifying again. Authority figures often had that effect on her. It was probably the reason she had never contradicted her mom and Sidney's mom when they had plotted her and Sidney's wedding.

"Please come in," said Charlene, stepping aside to allow them to enter her office.

For a moment Sharona didn't know how to greet the woman on whose benevolence her future depended. And since she only had a limited time frame to express herself, and three options momentarily vied for prevalence in her overwrought brain, for some reason she opted for a curtsy, as if Charlene Butterwick was the queen of Hampton Cove.

Charlene gave her an odd look, but then Sharona told herself it could have been worse. She could have kissed her on the cheek instead, which had been option number three. In hindsight option number one, a handshake, would probably have been more appropriate. Or not.

They walked through to the inner office of the ruler of Hampton Cove and stood around, waiting for the Mayor to give them permission to sit.

Charlene followed them in and carefully closed the door.

Sharona glanced around and saw that the office of their overlord and master was one of those old-fashioned wood-paneled rooms, with lots of portraits of men with mustaches on the walls. The windows were of the stained-glass variety, and offered an excellent view of the square in front of Town Hall. Sharona wondered if there was also a balcony where the Mayor could wave at her constituents gathered below and give rousing speeches.

But then the Mayor told them to take a seat and so they did.

"So," said Charlene as she folded her hands on her desk and studied them intently for a moment. "The Lucifer Committee."

"Coalition," Sharona muttered nervously.

Charlene frowned at her. "What did you say?"

"We're actually called the Lucifer Coalition, not the…"

Charlene's eyes narrowed, and Sharona decided it might be best if she shut up. "So what progress have you made?" the Mayor asked.

"Um…" Sidney glanced at the others, wordlessly asking permission to speak first. Sharona and Julius nodded, so he launched into the story of the military base sounding like a great place to relocate the mice to.

Charlene studied them for a moment, then nodded. "Great minds think alike, for last night the entire mouse colony, seemingly out of the blue, decided to pack up and leave the old Lucifer Match Factory and took up residence at the army base. In the process they also managed to attract the attention of our police force to the presence of a gang of drug smugglers, who were subsequently placed under arrest. As you can imagine, the Ministry of Defense wasn't too well pleased when they heard the news, and they have decided to finally evacuate the base and transfer ownership to the town of Hampton Cove to do with as we please." She smiled. "So I would like to give you a new assignment. Think up ways and means of using this wonderful piece of property in a way that will benefit our local community. I'm thinking social housing, recreational activities, turning it into a nature reserve, or all of the above. But please bear in mind that the mouse colony will have to live side by side with whatever you come up with as the new purpose for the base."

"Oh, that's so great," said Sharona, piping up. "So the mice are saved, and we get free rein to redevelop the base?"

"That's right," said Charlene. "So give it some thought, and I expect your ideas on my desk in a week." When their faces sagged, she said, "Let's make it two." Sidney had gingerly raised his hand. "Yes, Sidney?"

"Um… this is an old army base, so… so it stands to reason there will be weapons, right? I mean, guns and… and bombs and… and maybe nuclear… I mean, nuclear bombs, maybe?"

Charlene didn't laugh. Instead she said, "You know, that's actually a good question, Sidney."

"Thanks, Madam Mayor," Sidney murmured deferentially.

"I asked the same question. And the representative of the Ministry of Defense assured me that when the base was abandoned all the stockpiles of weapons that were present—if there ever were any weapons, that is, since that kind of information is classified—were removed. And when I asked him about the nuclear bombs he said there were never any nuclear bombs on site." She paused. "And if there were, they're gone now."

"Phew," said Sidney. "Oh, God, that's such a relief. Imagine a bunch of mice nibbling on some nuclear bomb and accidentally setting the thing off. That would be bad news, right?"

"Yes, Sidney," said Sharona. "A nuclear bomb going off in Hampton Cove would probably be bad news."

But Sidney didn't pick up on the note of sarcasm in her voice. Instead he was grinning from ear to ear. And now that his darkest fears had been allayed, he suddenly became talkative. "I really thought you were going to fire us, you know, Madam Mayor. So this is such a relief!"

"And why did you think that?" asked the Mayor.

Sharona gave Sidney's foot a kick, but of course he simply blundered on. "Oh, because we haven't actually done anything about that whole mouse project, I guess. I mean, Sharona came up with the idea about the army base, but then she met Julius and the two of them really hit it off, and then of course I met Chloe, and we've been practice-dating, and that turned into actual dating and now I'm proud to say we're an item, and Sharona and Julius are also an item, so I guess we've been so busy we more or less neglected our duties so…" Belatedly he realized he was digging his own grave and suddenly clamped his teeth together with a resounding click.

For a moment no one spoke. Then the Mayor said, "So Julius, you and Sharona?"

Both Julius and Sharona nodded, giving the Mayor sheepish looks.

"And Sidney, you and…"

"Chloe Gibson," said Sidney quietly, staring at his feet now as his face had turned the color of ripe beets.

"Well, that's great news, isn't it? It's always gratifying for me as your mayor to hear that your love lives are flourishing."

Sharona looked up at the Mayor with a frown, trying to detect the irony, but to her surprise she found none. On the contrary, the Mayor actually looked happy for them.

"I've always been of the opinion that a happy worker is a productive and efficient worker," said Charlene. "So the fact that all three of you are dating is great news and will, I'm sure, benefit our community." She smiled. "So when you're ready to distribute wedding invitations, let me know. I'll be more than happy to officiate the weddings personally."

"So… you're not mad?" asked Sidney finally.

"Mad? Why would I be mad? I think you came up with a great location for the mice, and as a consequence Hampton Cove will have the added benefit of a nice new park, or recreation zone or whatever you come up with. And I have every confidence that you will come up with something brilliant." She beamed. "Do you have any questions for me?"

"No," Sharona said. "No questions."

"That's great. Then I'll let you get back to work."

"I have a question, actually," said Julius.

"Shoot," said the Mayor pleasantly.

"How did the mice know that the army base was the spot we had picked? I mean, it's a fair distance away from that match factory. So how did they know where to go and how to get there?"

The Mayor gave him a serious nod. "I think that's one of those mysteries we'll probably never know the answer to, Julius."

Suddenly Sharona flashed back to Odelia Kingsley's cats for some reason, and remembered a persistent rumor she had once heard that they were able to communicate with their humans somehow. At the time she had discounted the rumor as belonging to the land of fairy tales. But now she wasn't so sure. Had the cats overheard them talking about the old army base? And had they somehow relayed that information to the mice? It all sounded pretty fantastical to her, but when she happened to look into the Mayor's eyes for a moment, she saw that Charlene was studying her closely, then gave her an almost imperceptible nod.

Of course. The Mayor was Alec Lip's girlfriend, and Alec was Odelia's uncle. Suddenly the whole thing made perfect sense. And when she glanced up at the Mayor once again, she saw that the woman had placed her index finger to her lips in the universal sign of discretion.

So she nodded and smiled. Oh, I'll keep quiet, she thought.

Who would believe such a crazy story anyway?

CHAPTER 32

*I*t hadn't taken us long to climb up on the porch swing and settle in. Our family was cooking up a storm, or I should probably say that Tex Poole was cooking up a storm. The doctor was master of his own domain, which currently consisted of his beloved barbecue set, where he was grilling something that smelled terrifically delicious. Next to me Dooley lay, and also Brutus and Harriet. All in all it had been an eventful couple of days, and now that everything was settled, both on the mouse front and the human front, I have to say I was happy that it was all over.

"So that drug gang, are they going to be all right?" asked Dooley.

"I hope not," Brutus grumbled. As the representative of the forces of law and order in our local cat community, being the cat of a cop, he didn't take kindly to a bunch of criminals using our lovely little town for their narcotic experiments.

"They'll be fine," I said. The gangsters had all been taken to the hospital where their wounds would be dressed and their sutures covered in ointment and generally be nursed back to health, at which point they would be transferred to the federal prison system that would have a nice couple of jail cells at their disposal for a lengthy period of time.

"I don't think we'll ever see any drug gangs around here again," said Harriet. "They probably learned their lesson."

"Oh, but these people are stubborn," I said. "I'm sure they'll try again, so we have to stay vigilant, you guys."

"We're always vigilant, Max," said Dooley, who had adopted a vigilant stance and was ready to face any criminals, great or small, and vanquish them in due course.

"So what happened to Barry Spence?" asked Harriet. "Will he have to go to prison?"

"Well, considering he murdered his wife and kids, I'd say that's probably a safe assumption," I said.

"Poor Mr. Spence," said Dooley. "Not only did he lose his family, but now he'll have to spend the rest of his life in prison."

"Less of the 'poor Mr. Spence,'" said Brutus sternly. "The man is nothing but an ordinary murderer in my book."

"Yeah, but he's also to be pitied in some way," said Harriet. "He did feel very bad about his wife leaving him and taking the kids."

"That's no excuse," Brutus grumbled. "If every person whose spouse is threatening to leave them would drive them into a lake, society would completely break down."

"It would be bad business for divorce lawyers, too," said Dooley as he gave this statement some thought. "They wouldn't have any clients left."

"Considering that there are almost seven hundred thousand divorces every year in this country alone," I said, having looked up the statistics, "that would mean a lot of murders."

"Let's hope Krystal manages to get past this ordeal," said Harriet, who felt for the poor nurse who had unwittingly fallen for a murderer.

"I'm sure she'll get over Barry," I said. As Odelia had told us the story, Krystal had been most cooperative once she had understood what kind of person she was harboring under her roof. Odelia had told us that she got the impression that Krystal had known somehow. Perhaps it was because she was a mother herself, but when Odelia told her what she thought was going on, she hadn't been that surprised.

"So how did you find out, Max?" asked Harriet.

"It seemed like a safe assumption that Barry was the person responsible," I said. "Considering what Silvester told us about it being a school night, why would Barry be driving around with his wife and kids in the car? And then of course there were Susan's suspicions against the man, and her absolute certainty Allison did not have an affair with her student."

"Also the lack of evidence that Barry was selling his company's secrets," Dooley suggested. "Isn't that right, Max?"

"Absolutely correct, Dooley."

I hadn't known for sure, of course, which is where Krystal came in. As Odelia had safely assumed, she was the only one who could get at the truth, considering her personal relationship with Barry.

Odelia walked over to give us some fresh nuggets straight from her dad's grill, and we gobbled them up with relish.

"This is just the best time of the week, isn't it?" said Harriet as she eagerly tucked into her delicacy.

"Yeah, it is," I agreed wholeheartedly.

"I hope Lucifer and his family will be fine," said Dooley, who had been worrying about the presence of nuclear weapons at that former army base again. "I've told him not to nibble on anything that looks suspicious, and he assured me he will spread the message to the rest of the clan. But it's hard, you know. You know what kids are like. They ignore the advice of their elders and instead go looking for adventure."

"Dooley, for the last time, there are no nuclear bombs on that base."

Dooley smiled. "Okay, I believe you, Max. No bombs. Gotcha."

Just then, in the distance a bomb seemed to go off. There was a loud sound like an explosion and we all jumped about a foot in the air.

"It's the nuclear bomb!" Dooley cried. "See? I knew I was right!"

Lucky for us it turned out to be a car backfiring. And so soon life went on, and all those present in the backyard of Marge and Tex laughed. Except for Dooley, who was on the lookout for a mushroom cloud. The only mushrooms present were the ones Gran had prepared for our barbecue, though, and as we all relaxed and enjoyed each other's company, the conversation drifted this way and that, as conversations often do.

Charlene spoke about some members of her administration who had announced their intention to get married, and how happy she was for them. She directed a curious glance at Uncle Alec when she mentioned the word 'marriage,' but Odelia's uncle blithely ignored her subtle hints.

At least until Gran said, "So when are you two going to tie the knot, huh? Alec? Have you popped the question yet?"

Uncle Alec looked like a deer caught in the headlights, causing all those around the table to laugh heartily. The intrepid cop seemed more scared of walking down the aisle than of catching a brace of hardened criminals.

He swallowed convulsively. "I... I mean... I mean it's..."

"Oh, Alec," said Charlene coyly. "You've got such a way with words. You make this girl go all gooey inside."

"Just spit it out, son," Gran urged. "I've raised you better than that. It's not rocket science. 'Do you want to marry me?' See? It's not hard."

"Um…" Uncle Alec looked this way and that, except at his girlfriend, and Charlene giggled. "It's just that…" He swallowed some more, his Adam's apple dancing the mambo in his throat. Before finally glancing in our direction, hoping to find inspiration with the four of us.

"Just do it, Uncle Alec," was Harriet's advice.

"Yeah, you won't regret it," was Brutus's opinion.

"Go for it, big guy," said Dooley happily.

"You'll be very happy together," was my contribution.

Uncle Alec glanced at his niece uncertainly, but when Odelia translated our words, he didn't look overjoyed, as one would expect.

For a moment silence reigned. It's one thing if a man is too timid to propose, but it's another if he simply refuses to do the deed. It points to a deeper underlying issue, like the fact that he's secretly in love with someone else. And this clearly was what Charlene was starting to suspect, as her expression turned a little sad. I could see she was distressed.

"It's fine," said Gran, who realized what turmoil she had caused with her ill-advised comment. "You don't have to decide now, Alec. You've got all the time in the world."

"But I don't, do I?" said Uncle Alec, looking pained. "I'm not getting any younger, and frankly I don't…"

"It's all right," said Charlene, looking away. "You don't… I mean, forget about it, Alec. We always said we weren't going to have any expectations going into this, so…"

"No, but I want you to have expectations," said Alec, and I could see he was struggling. "It's just that… I want you to be happy, Charlene, since you're such a great person. The best person I have ever met in my life. And frankly I ask myself every day what you're doing with me, you know. Not that I don't thank my lucky stars, cause I do. It's just that…"

"Yes?" asked Charlene, casting a hopeful glance at her boyfriend.

"It's just that you can do so much better than me. I mean, there are so many guys out there that are so much better for you than I could ever be. More handsome, more eloquent, more intelligent, with more money…"

Charlene gave him a smile. "But I don't want another guy, Alec. All I want is you, you know."

Uncle Alec suddenly produced a sort of sob. "I love you, honey. I mean… I love you so, so much…"

"I love you, my big huggy bear."

And suddenly, and much to everyone's surprise, Alec seemed to tumble from his chair. There was a gasp of shock, but then we saw he had actually gone down on one knee and was gazing hopefully into Charlene's face. "I don't have a ring," he announced.

"That's my fault," said Gran. "I'm sorry. Me and my big mouth."

"Charlene Butterwick, will you take me, Alec Lip, to be your lawfully wedded wife—I mean husband?"

Charlene had clasped her hands together and looked really touched by this gesture from her 'huggy bear.'

"Yes," she finally said. "A thousand times yes!"

"Oh, dear," said Marge, wiping away a tear.

Tex had stepped away from his grill set and asked, "What's going on? What did I miss?"

"Oh, just that you're losing a brother-in-law and gaining a sister-in-law," said Gran. "Though that's probably not entirely correct, is it?"

"Oh, Gran," Dooley laughed. "You're so funny."

There was kissing going on, and so Brutus and Harriet and I averted Dooley's eyes. But our friend pushed our paws away. "I've seen people kiss, you guys. It's fine. It's what people do when they're in love."

"This is so great," said Scarlett, who had filmed the whole scene with her phone. "I think I've got the whole thing."

"Of course you have," said Gran happily. I could see that her eyes were moist and it was clear that she was very touched by the touching scene. "Now go and make me some grandkids," she exhorted. And when Charlene laughed, she added, "I'm not kidding, Madam Mayor!"

"I hope she's kidding," said Harriet. "Can you imagine Uncle Alec as a dad?"

"I can, actually," I said. "And I think he'd be a great dad."

We studied the police chief's face, and saw that he had probably never looked happier. And who knows? Maybe his union with Charlene would be blessed with kids. The world is a wonderful place, and life likes to spring these little surprises on you from time to time. And there was at least one other proponent of more babies being born and that was Odelia and Chase's daughter Grace.

She had climbed up on the swing and had plunked herself down next to us. "I hope they have babies," she revealed. "It's not a lot of fun being the only baby in the family, you know. I could use some company."

"Oh, but there's plenty of babies in the family," I said. "There's Tex."

We looked over and saw that he was sampling his own wares, decided they were excellent, and hopped back to his grill to whip up some more goodies.

"And there's Gran," I continued.

The old lady was actually coming up with names for Alec and Charlene's baby and the one she liked the most was Vesta, whether it was a boy or a girl—she didn't care.

"You know what I mean, Max," said Grace. "An actual baby I can play with."

"I know," I said.

"For now you'll just have to play with us," said Dooley.

"Thanks, Dooley," she said, and gave him a big hug.

As we all relaxed, the party in full swing, for a moment I

thought I saw a mouse tripping through the backyard and trying to draw my attention. But this time I decided to ignore it. To be perfectly honest I wasn't looking forward to relocating another twenty million mice. Even cat detectives are entitled to some peace and quiet from time to time.

For me that time was now. And so I promptly dozed off.

THE END

Thanks for reading! If you want to know when a new Nic Saint book comes out, sign up for Nic's mailing list: nicsaint.com/news

ABOUT NIC

Nic has a background in political science and before being struck by the writing bug worked odd jobs around the world (including but not limited to massage therapist in Mexico, gardener in Italy, restaurant manager in India, and Berlitz teacher in Belgium).

When he's not writing he enjoys curling up with a good (comic) book, watching British crime dramas, French comedies or Nancy Meyers movies, sampling pastry (apple cake!), pasta and chocolate (preferably the dark variety), twisting himself into a pretzel doing morning yoga, going for a run, and spoiling his big red tomcat Tommy.

He lives with his wife (and aforementioned cat) in a small village smack dab in the middle of absolutely nowhere and is probably writing his next 'Mysteries of Max' book right now.

www.nicsaint.com

ALSO BY NIC SAINT

The Mysteries of Max

Purrfect Murder

Purrfectly Deadly

Purrfect Revenge

Purrfect Heat

Purrfect Crime

Purrfect Rivalry

Purrfect Peril

Purrfect Secret

Purrfect Alibi

Purrfect Obsession

Purrfect Betrayal

Purrfectly Clueless

Purrfectly Royal

Purrfect Cut

Purrfect Trap

Purrfectly Hidden

Purrfect Kill

Purrfect Boy Toy

Purrfectly Dogged

Purrfectly Dead

Purrfect Saint

Purrfect Advice

Purrfect Passion

A Purrfect Gnomeful

Purrfect Cover

Purrfect Patsy

Purrfect Son

Purrfect Fool

Purrfect Fitness

Purrfect Setup

Purrfect Sidekick

Purrfect Deceit

Purrfect Ruse

Purrfect Swing

Purrfect Cruise

Purrfect Harmony

Purrfect Sparkle

Purrfect Cure

Purrfect Cheat

Purrfect Catch

Purrfect Design

Purrfect Life

Purrfect Thief

Purrfect Crust

Purrfect Bachelor

Purrfect Double

Purrfect Date

Purrfect Hit

Purrfect Baby

Purrfect Mess

Purrfect Paris

Purrfect Model

Purrfect Slug

Purrfect Match

Purrfect Game

Purrfect Bouquet

Purrfect Home

Purrfectly Slim

Purrfect Nap

Purrfect Yacht

Purrfect Scam

Purrfect Fury

Purrfect Christmas

Purrfect Gems

Purrfect Demons

The Mysteries of Max Collections

Collection 1 (Books 1-3)

Collection 2 (Books 4-6)

Collection 3 (Books 7-9)

Collection 4 (Books 10-12)

Collection 5 (Books 13-15)

Collection 6 (Books 16-18)

Collection 7 (Books 19-21)

Collection 8 (Books 22-24)

Collection 9 (Books 25-27)

Collection 10 (Books 28-30)

Collection 11 (Books 31-33)

Collection 12 (Books 34-36)

Collection 13 (Books 37-39)

The Mysteries of Max Big Collections

The Mysteries of Max Short Stories

Nora Steel

Murder Retreat

The Kellys

Murder Motel

Death in Suburbia

Emily Stone

Murder at the Art Class

Washington & Jefferson

First Shot

Alice Whitehouse

Spooky Times

Spooky Trills

Spooky End

Spooky Spells

Ghosts of London

Between a Ghost and a Spooky Place

Public Ghost Number One

Ghost Save the Queen

Box Set 1 (Books 1-3)

A Tale of Two Harrys

Ghost of Girlband Past

Ghostlier Things

Charleneland

Deadly Ride

Final Ride

Neighborhood Witch Committee

Witchy Start

Witchy Worries

Witchy Wishes

Saffron Diffley

Crime and Retribution

Vice and Verdict

Felonies and Penalties (Saffron Diffley Short 1)

The B-Team

Once Upon a Spy

Tate-à-Tate

Enemy of the Tates

Ghosts vs. Spies

The Ghost Who Came in from the Cold

Witchy Fingers

Witchy Trouble

Witchy Hexations

Witchy Possessions

Witchy Riches

Box Set 1 (Books 1-4)

The Mysteries of Bell & Whitehouse

One Spoonful of Trouble

Two Scoops of Murder

Three Shots of Disaster

Box Set 1 (Books 1-3)

A Twist of Wraith

A Touch of Ghost

A Clash of Spooks

Box Set 2 (Books 4-6)

The Stuffing of Nightmares

A Breath of Dead Air

An Act of Hodd

Box Set 3 (Books 7-9)

A Game of Dons

Standalone Novels

When in Bruges

The Whiskered Spy

ThrillFix

Made in the USA
Las Vegas, NV
06 November 2023

80344009R00135